If She Heard

BOOKS BY BLAKE PIERCE

ADELE SHARP MYSTERY SERIES

LEFT TO DIE (Book #1)
LEFT TO RUN (Book #2)
LEFT TO HIDE (Book #3)

THE AU PAIR SERIES

ALMOST GONE (Book#1)
ALMOST LOST (Book #2)
ALMOST DEAD (Book #3)

ZOE PRIME MYSTERY SERIES

FACE OF DEATH (Book#1)
FACE OF MURDER (Book #2)
FACE OF FEAR (Book #3)
FACE OF MADNESS (Book #4)

A JESSIE HUNT PSYCHOLOGICAL SUSPENSE SERIES

THE PERFECT WIFE (Book #1)
THE PERFECT BLOCK (Book #2)
THE PERFECT HOUSE (Book #3)
THE PERFECT SMILE (Book #4)
THE PERFECT LIE (Book #5)
THE PERFECT LOOK (Book #6)
THE PERFECT AFFAIR (Book #7)

CHLOE FINE PSYCHOLOGICAL SUSPENSE SERIES

NEXT DOOR (Book #1)
A NEIGHBOR'S LIE (Book #2)
CUL DE SAC (Book #3)

SILENT NEIGHBOR (Book #4)
HOMECOMING (Book #5)
TINTED WINDOWS (Book #6)

KATE WISE MYSTERY SERIES

IF SHE KNEW (Book #1)
IF SHE SAW (Book #2)
IF SHE RAN (Book #3)
IF SHE HID (Book #4)
IF SHE FLED (Book #5)
IF SHE FEARED (Book #6)
IF SHE HEARD (Book #7)

THE MAKING OF RILEY PAIGE SERIES

WATCHING (Book #1)
WAITING (Book #2)
LURING (Book #3)
TAKING (Book #4)
STALKING (Book #5)
KILLING (Book #6)

RILEY PAIGE MYSTERY SERIES

ONCE GONE (Book #1)
ONCE TAKEN (Book #2)
ONCE CRAVED (Book #3)
ONCE LURED (Book #4)
ONCE HUNTED (Book #5)
ONCE PINED (Book #6)
ONCE FORSAKEN (Book #7)
ONCE COLD (Book #8)
ONCE STALKED (Book #9)
ONCE LOST (Book #10)
ONCE BURIED (Book #11)
ONCE BOUND (Book #12)
ONCE TRAPPED (Book #13)

ONCE DORMANT (Book #14)
ONCE SHUNNED (Book #15)
ONCE MISSED (Book #16)
ONCE CHOSEN (Book #17)

MACKENZIE WHITE MYSTERY SERIES

BEFORE HE KILLS (Book #1)
BEFORE HE SEES (Book #2)
BEFORE HE COVETS (Book #3)
BEFORE HE TAKES (Book #4)
BEFORE HE NEEDS (Book #5)
BEFORE HE FEELS (Book #6)
BEFORE HE SINS (Book #7)
BEFORE HE HUNTS (Book #8)
BEFORE HE PREYS (Book #9)
BEFORE HE LONGS (Book #10)
BEFORE HE LAPSES (Book #11)
BEFORE HE ENVIES (Book #12)
BEFORE HE STALKS (Book #13)
BEFORE HE HARMS (Book #14)

AVERY BLACK MYSTERY SERIES

CAUSE TO KILL (Book #1)
CAUSE TO RUN (Book #2)
CAUSE TO HIDE (Book #3)
CAUSE TO FEAR (Book #4)
CAUSE TO SAVE (Book #5)
CAUSE TO DREAD (Book #6)

KERI LOCKE MYSTERY SERIES

A TRACE OF DEATH (Book #1)
A TRACE OF MUDER (Book #2)
A TRACE OF VICE (Book #3)
A TRACE OF CRIME (Book #4)
A TRACE OF HOPE (Book #5)

If She Heard

(A Kate Wise Mystery—Book 7)

Blake Pierce

BLAKE PIERCE

Blake Pierce is the USA Today bestselling author of the RILEY PAGE mystery series, which includes seventeen books. Blake Pierce is also the author of the MACKENZIE WHITE mystery series, comprising thirteen books (and counting); of the AVERY BLACK mystery series, comprising six books; of the KERI LOCKE mystery series, comprising five books; of the MAKING OF RILEY PAIGE mystery series, comprising six books; of the KATE WISE mystery series, comprising seven books; of the CHLOE FINE psychological suspense mystery, comprising six books; of the JESSE HUNT psychological suspense thriller series, comprising seven books (and counting); of the AU PAIR psychological suspense thriller series, comprising two books (and counting); of the ZOE PRIME mystery series, comprising three books (and counting); and of the new ADELE SHARP mystery series.

ONCE GONE (a Riley Paige Mystery—Book #1), BEFORE HE KILLS (A Mackenzie White Mystery—Book 1), CAUSE TO KILL (An Avery Black Mystery—Book 1), A TRACE OF DEATH (A Keri Locke Mystery—Book 1), WATCHING (The Making of Riley Paige—Book 1), NEXT DOOR (A Chloe Fine Psychological Suspense Mystery—Book 1), THE PERFECT WIFE (A Jessie Hunt Psychological Suspense Thriller—Book One), and IF SHE KNEW (A Kate Wise Mystery—Book 1) are each available as a free download on Amazon!

An avid reader and lifelong fan of the mystery and thriller genres, Blake loves to hear from you, so please feel free to visit www.blakepierceauthor.com to learn more and stay in touch.

Table of Contents

Chapter One

Even before the baby arrived, people were calling Kate Wise the Miracle Mother. Upon learning that she was going to be giving birth at the age of fifty-seven, Kate had told no one other than Allen and Melissa. She hadn't even told anyone at work. Not DeMarco, not Duran . . . no one. But somehow, word had gotten out. By the time she was five months pregnant, everyone at the bureau knew about it and there were journalists and reporters calling.

Oddly enough, the first journalist who had called her was on her mind as the doctor checked to see how much she was dilated. She'd found the idea of her pregnancy being newsworthy a little ridiculous. But as her doctors had told her and as some Google research had verified, it was rare for a woman beyond fifty to get pregnant—and even more rare for that woman to carry the baby to full term.

But here she was, her water having broken eight hours ago, with her doctor telling her she was eight centimeters dilated and it was almost time.

The first reporter had been a woman from *Mother and Baby* magazine. Kate had only taken the call out of a need to not be rude. They'd spoken on the phone twice; the second call ended up being more focused on her ability to maintain a second career within the FBI. The reporter had spoken to her as if Kate were some sort of superhero. Kate had never known why, but something about the interview had sat wrong with her for the entirety of her pregnancy.

Because no one should look to me as an example, Kate thought as another contraction went tearing through her more-than-half-a-century-old body. *This is torture.*

She did not remember her pregnancy with Melissa being this hard. Of course, that had been almost thirty years ago. That had been planned, and there had been no reporters. There had been no thirty-second blips on the evening news about her pregnancy, no nicknames like Miracle Mother to live up to.

"Kate?" the doctor said. His voice tore her out of her thoughts, managing to find a way in through the pain of the latest contraction. "You still with me?"

"Uh-huh."

It was true, though the world was something of a haze. The pregnancy was high risk. There had been issues from the fourth month on. Worries of low birth weight, a scare where the baby's heartbeat had been far too slow, and now here he was, three weeks early and projected to weigh about a pound and a half under what the doctor considered safe.

"He's here, Kate. I need you to push, okay? One more big push and your baby boy will be—"

Kate pushed, and the room spun. She was vaguely aware of Allen by her side. He was holding her hand, his face next to hers as he coached her on and encouraged her. Kate let out a moan, doing everything she could not to scream. The world started growing dim just as she heard the first cries of her newborn baby son.

Her vision was hazy at best when the doctor placed her son on her chest. She cradled him in her arms and started to cry. She hated the word *miracle,* as it was tossed around far too often. But feeling the warmth of her baby in her arms, held against her nearly sixty-year-old body, she supposed that's what this was . . . a miracle.

It was a nice thought to hang on to as exhaustion swept over her and her vision went from hazy to a complete and perfect field of black.

⚜ ⚜ ⚜

In the coming weeks, Kate was overcome with a huge wave of depression. Now that her son was here—named Michael, after her late husband—she started to obsess over the negatives of being a new mother at the age of fifty-seven. First of all, she had to accept the fact that in the past eighteen months, she had become both a grandmother *and* a new mother. There was also the fact that by the time this new kid was old enough to go to college, she'd be pushing eighty. And thinking of college opened her eyes to the added expense. She had enough money saved up, but she had made plans for it—namely a lot of traveling after sixty. But now those plans would have to change.

She also wondered how Allen was going to truly handle it all. Sure, he had been great so far. He had been genuinely excited through most of the pregnancy, but now the baby was actually here and changing their lives . . . especially Allen's. First of all, Michael had stayed in the hospital for three weeks. He'd been in NICU while a team of doctors made sure he was going to gain weight. Kate missed most of this, as her own recovery was much harder than she'd expected. The strain of the birth had thrown her back out and her femoral nerves had also been damaged, causing her to occasionally lose feeling in her legs. She was finally officially released from the hospital after eleven days.

Twenty days after he was born, Michael was allowed to go home. He weighed five pounds seven ounces when Kate rested him in his bassinet for the first time. For the two days that followed, Kate had been an almost obsessive mother. She'd make sure he was breathing at least five times during each of his naps and at night; she hovered over Allen when he held their son, and she would not even let Melissa hold him.

Those two days had worn her out and that, she supposed, was what brought the depression on. She stayed in bed for eight full days, only getting up to use the bathroom and to shower on three occasions. Allen was essentially a single parent in that time, and during one of her nights of being holed up in her bed, Kate heard him sobbing.

On that eighth day, it was Melissa of all people who convinced her to get out of bed. There was a knock at the bedroom door. She assumed it was Allen and answered with a groggy "Come in."

When she saw that it was Melissa, she wanted to cry but wasn't sure why. She propped herself up on her left elbow, surprised at how much it hurt to do so. Staying in bed had made her quite sore.

"Lissa," she said. "What a surprise."

Melissa sat on the edge of the bed and took her mother's hand. "How you doing, Mom?"

"I don't know," she answered honestly. "Tired. Wiped out. Depressed."

"Still having issues with your legs?"

"No, they seem okay. Haven't lost feeling in them since I got back home."

"Good. Knowing your legs are okay is going to make me seem like less of a bully with what I say next."

"What is it?" Kate asked.

"I love you, Mom. But it's time to get your ass out of bed."

"I want to, I really do. But I—"

"No, Mom. Allen has been busting his ass this past week. I've helped where I can, but he only lets me do so much because he's afraid of how you'll react. Look…I get how weird and scary this has to be, but you need to face it. You're fifty-seven and you just had a baby. And you survived it. Now it's time to be a mother. And I can tell you from personal experience that you're pretty good at it."

Kate sat up and looked sternly at her daughter. "Allen…is he okay?"

"No. He's exhausted and he's afraid you're in some bad place you won't come back from. But I told him to get that right out of his head. You're a rock star. He told me how you pushed through that pregnancy. And I've watched you reclaim a career as a female FBI agent even after you retired. You handled that…so you can handle this. More importantly, you were excited to start your career again at fifty-five. So now it's time to be excited for this baby at fifty-seven."

Kate nodded, and when the tears started to come, she did not fight them.

"There's just one thing I need to let you know," Melissa said.

"What's that?"

"If you need me to tell you how babies are made, I can do it. Seems to me at this age, you'd know how to be safe."

Kate burst out laughing. It hurt her sides, her stomach, and her head, but it also felt good at the same time. Melissa laughed right along with her, taking Kate's hand again. "I mean, for real. My daughter is older than her own uncle. How the hell does that even work?"

Kate laughed even louder and leaned into her daughter. They embraced and stayed that way for so long that after a while, Kate could not tell where the laughter stopped and the crying began.

Slowly, Melissa helped Kate out of bed. She coached her through getting in the shower and even put on a pot of tea while her mother washed off. Taking a shower, as simple as it was, helped to bring Kate around a lot. But, to her amazement, it was also exhausting. She felt like an invalid as she struggled to put her clothes on.

As she fought to get her arms into a T-shirt, Melissa came into the room and helped. "I don't know that I've ever helped you into your clothes," Melissa said. "Good thing I've had Michelle to practice on. I bet she never would have thought her grandmother would need help getting dressed."

"Were you always such a smart ass?" Kate asked.

"Always."

Together, they left the bedroom and walked into the living room. Kate looked around, amazed at how clean and quiet the place was. "Where's Allen and Michael?" she asked.

Allen took him out for a walk around the block. He's done it twice a day for the last three days."

"God, have I been *that* out?"

"You have." Melissa took the kettle off of the stove and poured hot water into waiting cups with tea bags in them. "Mom... are you going to be able to do this?"

"I think so. Eventually. It's just overwhelming. And it took way too much out of me."

"I thought I was going to die when I had Michelle. I can't imagine giving birth at your age." She smirked here and added: "You old fart."

"You know," Kate said, "somehow, it became much easier to be apart from you over the years."

This time it was Melissa who broke out laughing. It was like music to Kate. It warmed her heart in a way that she had missed. Sadly, she realized that she could not remember the last time she'd heard Melissa laugh so hard.

It made her wonder what else she had missed and taken for granted.

⚜ ⚜ ⚜

Director Duran kept his distance in the months that followed. He sent a card and a care package of diapers and wipes a week after Michael's birth, but refrained from any emails or phone calls. Kate appreciated the gesture but started to feel a creeping sort of certainty about her future with the bureau. Having a baby at the age of fifty-seven and becoming something of a local celebrity for it likely meant her brief resurgence at work was now over.

On the other hand, she couldn't help but wonder if the bureau might enjoy some of the free press. Not only free press, but uplifting and uncontroversial press for once.

She wished she could be fine with it, but she wasn't. She grew to love Michael more and more every day. There had been a few days where she had resented him, but it did not last long. After all, Melissa's speech had been accurate. Had she and Allen been more careful, she would not have gotten pregnant. Then again, the idea of being careful sexually when you were fifty-five tended to look different than it did for other dating adults.

Three months after she had been coaxed out of bed by Melissa, Kate was able to see this last stretch of her life for what it was. It would be a life of domestication and learning how to be a mother again. It would be learning how to love and trust a man with not only her life, but the life of their child.

Ultimately, she was fine with it. Hell, she was sure there were some grandmothers who would do anything to experience that feeling of being a new mother again. And here she was, with that chance.

Allen seemed fine with it as well. They had not yet talked about what the rest of their lives would look like in terms of marriage and co-parenting. He was still loving her well and seemed absolutely nuts about little Michael, but he seemed timid a lot of the time. It was like he was running underneath a cliff, waiting to be brained by a boulder that was sure to fall on him at any moment.

She wasn't sure what was bothering him until her phone rang on a Wednesday afternoon. Kate was sitting on the couch with Michael. Allen picked the phone up from the kitchen counter and brought it to her. He wasn't necessarily spying when he looked down to see the display; it was just something they did now, a level of comfort she had been totally fine with.

Yet when he handed the phone to her, he had a sour expression on his face. She took the phone, he took Michael from her, and she looked to the display as she answered the call.

It was Duran.

Kate and Allen locked eyes for a moment and she understood his strain.

Her heart racing, Kate answered the call.

Allen walked into the kitchen; the shadow of that falling boulder may as well have been growing larger and larger, covering him completely.

Chapter Two

Sandra Peterson woke up fifteen minutes before her alarm was set to go off. She had been waking up to that same alarm, at 6:30 every morning, for the last two years or so. She'd always been a good sleeper, managing seven to nine hours every night and never waking before the alarm. But this morning, she was stirred awake by excitement. Kayla was home from college and they were going to spend the entire day together.

It would be the first time they'd spent more than half a day together since Kayla started college last year. She was home because one of her childhood friends was getting married. Kayla had been raised in Harper Hills, North Carolina, a small rural town about twenty miles outside of Charlotte, and had opted to enroll in an out-of-state college as early as she could. Going to school at Florida State meant their times together were few and far between. They'd last seen each other at Christmas, and that had been almost a year ago for only a period of ten hours before Kayla had left to visit her father in Tennessee.

Kayla had always handled the divorce well. Sandra and her husband had split when Kayla was eleven and she never really even seemed to care. Sandra supposed it was one of the reasons Kayla had never played favorites. When she visited one parent, she made a point to visit the other. And because of that torturous trip—from Tallahassee, to Harper Hills, to Nashville—Kayla didn't visit very often.

Sandra shuffled out of the bedroom in her pajamas and bedroom slippers. She walked down the hallway toward the kitchen, passing by Kayla's room. She didn't expect her daughter to wake up any time before eight, and that was fine. Sandra figured she could put some coffee on and prepare a nice breakfast for when she was awake.

She did just that, scrambling up some eggs, frying some bacon, and making a dozen silver dollar pancakes. The kitchen was smelling amazing by seven o'clock, and Sandra was surprised the smells hadn't stirred Kayla awake yet. It had worked when Kayla had been at home, especially when the high school years had come about. But now the smells of her home cooking apparently did not have the same effect on her daughter.

Anyway, Kayla had been out with friends last night—some friends she hadn't seen since high school graduation. Sandra hadn't felt right sticking with her daughter's old curfew now that she was in college, so Sandra had simply left it at: *Come home in one piece and preferably sober.*

As the morning crept on toward eight and Kayla had still not come out of her room, Sandra started to worry. Rather than knock on the bedroom door and potentially wake her up, though, Sandra looked out the living room window. She saw Kayla's car in the driveway, parked right behind her own car.

Relieved, Sandra went back to making breakfast. When all of the food was ready, it was 7:55. Sandra hated to wake her daughter (she was sure it would be seen as rude and uncool), but she simply couldn't help it. Maybe after breakfast, Kayla would take a nap and rest up before they started their day of shopping and a late lunch in Charlotte. Besides . . . the eggs were going to get cold and Kayla had always made a point to mention how gross cold eggs were.

Sandra walked down the hall to Kayla's room. It felt surreal and comforting at the same time. How many times had she knocked on this door in her adult life? Thousands, for sure. To be doing it again made her heart warm.

She knocked, paused a moment, and then added a sweet-sounding: "Kayla, honey? Breakfast is ready."

There was no response from inside. Sandra frowned. She was not naïve enough to think that Kayla and her friends had not been drinking last night. She had never seen her daughter drunk or enduring a hangover and did not want to see it at all if she could help it. She wondered if Kayla was simply hungover and not ready to face her mother.

"There's coffee," Sandra added, hoping it might help.

Still no response. She knocked one more time, louder this time, and opened the door.

The bed was still perfectly made. There was no sign of Kayla.

But that makes no sense, Sandra thought. *Her car is out front.*

She then recalled a particularly ungraceful moment from her own teenage years where she had driven home drunk out of her mind. She'd managed to make it home but had passed out in her car, in the driveway. She found it hard to imagine Kayla behaving in such a way but there were only so many other possibilities to consider.

As Sandra closed Kayla's bedroom door and walked back through the kitchen, a little ball of worry bounced around in her stomach. Maybe Kayla had been hiding some drinking or drug problems from her. Maybe they'd spend their day talking through such things rather than their planned day of fun.

Sandra steeled up her courage to have such a conversation as she opened the front door. Just as she stepped out onto the porch, she froze. Her left leg literally paused in the air, refusing to set down.

Because if she set her foot down, she was stepping into a new world—a world where what she saw on her front porch was going to have to be faced and accepted.

Kayla was lying on the porch. She was on her back and staring up with unblinking eyes. There were red abrasions around her throat. She was not moving.

Sandra finally brought that other foot down. When she did, the rest of her body followed it. She fell into a crumpled ball by her dead daughter, thoughts of breakfast and shopping completely forgotten.

Chapter Three

It never got any easier to step into a meeting with Director Duran. He had always been fair with Kate and she even considered him a good friend. But the nature of the call and the way the last few months of her life had gone made Kate think that this was going to be a tense meeting—perhaps a meeting that would put an end to her briefly resurrected career as an FBI agent.

When she stepped into his office, he greeted her with the no-nonsense smile she had come to know and appreciate ever since he had taken over for the director who had overseen the first half of her career. She and Duran were roughly the same age (she had never bothered to ask how old he was because it seemed rude) and had a mutual appreciation for one another.

"Hey, Kate, have a seat."

She was immediately alarmed that he had used her first name. It was very informal, something he had only ever done in after-hours situations or when conversations had gotten heated.

"Kate, huh?" she asked. She was beyond the point of being nervous around him. She made the comment in jest, as if basically painting the situation for what it was and placing it neatly on the desk between them.

"Well, as far as I'm concerned, you're still on your extended maternity leave," he said. "Seemed silly to call you agent. However, as you might have imagined, all of that is sort of why I wanted to speak with you." He let out a deep breath here and looked her straight in the eyes. "How are you, Kate?"

"Good. Confused, I guess."

"Feeling like the Miracle Mom?"

"I suppose I do fit right in with the celebrity circles, don't I?" she joked. "I need to hurry this up, by the way. I have a lunch scheduled with Ryan Seacrest right after this."

"I don't know who that is."

Kate shrugged. Humor had never really been a part of their relationship anyway.

"I won't lie," Duran said. "It was sort of cool around here. People quick to say they knew you. Sharing links and articles about the Miracle Mom."

"You know, I only did two interviews. How that turned into more than forty articles, I'll never know."

"That's social media for you. It was nuts. Anyway . . . tell me, Kate. Has your newfound fame made you think twice about returning to the bureau?"

She couldn't help but laugh. "No. If anything is going to keep me from coming back, it would not be my brush with fame."

"But something *could* stop you?"

"Maybe. My baby, for one. My age for another."

"You've been out for three months now," he said. "A little more, actually. I suppose I don't need to point out that you're not getting younger. Still . . . your body of work post-retirement is pretty impressive."

"Forgive me for being so blunt and to the point," Kate said. "But what do *you* want? Do you want me back?"

"In a perfect world, yes. But there have been meetings here and there. All of those articles not only highlight that you gave birth at fifty-seven, but that you are also still an active FBI agent. You go back out there, I don't know what that's going to be like in terms of media attention."

Kate reclined back in her seat. She hadn't even thought of that.

"Let's be real for a minute," Duran went on. "Yes, I want you back. But that's being selfish. You're a great asset and, if I'm being *very* real, it would do wonders for the bureau. The media loves you right now. You're like some weird C-list celebrity, right up there with those kids that react to new music on YouTube. But I'm not going to try to sway you. If you want out, you can have out and I think everyone would understand."

"I miss it, though," Kate said. She hadn't even fully realized it until it was out of her mouth.

"I figured you did. So what I can do—for the next few months, anyway—is set you on some low-risk cases. Just some things to keep your mind busy and your focus sharp. That is, if you feel that you've had enough time to rest and you're ready to head back out."

"I am," she said. The idea of placing Michael into daycare hurt her heart, but she knew it would be good for him... as well as for her and Allen. Though, if she were being honest, she wasn't sure she was quite ready for it yet. Before she could get dragged down by those thoughts, she carried on with the conversation. "How has DeMarco been doing? I've only spoken to her three times since I've been out and every time I asked her about work, she was quick to change the subject."

"That might be because she's been quite busy. I'm allowed to tell you because she's technically still listed as your partner... but she has been involved in two high-profile cases. Three weeks ago, she arrested two men who had been getting heroin out on the streets. A week before that, she single-handedly brought in a guy who killed three people in West Virginia and was on the run, passing through Maryland."

"Seems she *has* been busy."

"And now that you mention DeMarco, she's just been given a briefing on a case in North Carolina. Seems like a cut-and-dry stalker-type case. Two dead young women, college-aged. DeMarco is on a roll and I'm sure she'd love to have you back. If this one is as simple as it seems on paper, it could be a great fit for both of you, in your different situations."

"And what is my situation?"

"You know what I meant, Kate. If you want to try to get back into the swing of things, this might be a good case to do it. It is, of course, one hundred percent up to you."

"It sounds nice, but I don't want to get in her way if she's doing well for herself."

"I'm sure she'd love to have you. And, again sticking with honesty, if we don't know how much longer you're going to work, I think it makes more sense to have you paired with someone you know well."

"Makes sense."

Duran considered things for a moment before getting to his feet. "She's due to leave tomorrow morning. Does that give you and your husband enough time to sort things out? If you don't mind my asking, has it even been a conversation?"

"It has," she said. "Maybe an unspoken one, but it's been on our minds. I think he knows I'm not done, but..."

"But what?"

"But that it's close. That my time with the bureau is coming to an end."

There was another question on Duran's mind. She could see him debating whether or not to ask it. But she knew what it was and she was grateful he kept it quiet.

Is this your last case?

She was glad he left it unspoken because she had no idea how to answer it.

⚜ ⚜ ⚜

It was the sole topic of conversation at dinner. Allen took it well, mainly because he'd known it was coming. The moment Duran had called earlier in the day, he had known. The conversation had gone surprisingly well, though there was an underlying tension hovering over the dining room table.

"Here's the thing," Allen said, shoving his now-empty plate to the side. He'd made teriyaki chicken for dinner and it had been amazing. It was another of those small ways he treated her well. "There's a very large part of me that is thrilled you're going back. The last month or so, it's been almost painful to watch you stalking around the place, looking like you lost your keys and had no idea where to look for them. I know you miss it and in terms of this case, I'm happy to agree to it. But it raises some questions."

"A lot of questions," Kate agreed. "Let's tackle them."

"Great. While I am pretty much retired at this point, I *will* still have to take calls and attend meetings here and there for the next year or so to wrap up those last-minute deals. So I'll ask that your job not automatically overrule mine. That being said, we need to go ahead and pull the trigger on lining up daycare for Michael."

"Agreed. Now, for this case, are you open for the next week or so?"

"I am. I have nothing on the calendar for another three weeks, actually."

"And would you mind being a single father for several days if I take this case?"

"Sure thing. Boy time will be fun."

"What other questions do you have?"

"I'm thinking of the safety factor. I know you can hold your own and it's one of the reasons I love you. But I also don't like the idea of my fifty-seven-year-old wife out there chasing after men half her age that have no problem killing her. It's not like you're one of these agents that sit behind a desk or parked in a car."

"Duran and I talked about that. This case in particular should be a pretty simple one. He's also aware of the age factor, though he was a bit more pleasant about how he worded it."

"One more." Allen leaned back in his chair and took a sip of his wine. He looked over to the bouncy seat Michael had been snoozing in while they ate and smiled. "How long are you going to keep at it? Honestly? How much longer can you push it? I can't imagine putting your body through the stress of having a child has made it any easier."

"It's a difficult question to answer," she said. "This whole situation . . . I could have never dreamed it up. A baby at fifty-seven. A supervisor and a partner who still want me active. It's more than I can honestly wrap my head around and . . . I just don't know. I don't think I will until I get back out there."

She watched how he thought about it, how the right corner of his mouth ticked down into an almost-frown the way it often did when he was deep in thought.

"Then I think you need to get back out there," he said. "For now. Maybe we revisit this in three months and see what it looks like. Does that seem fair?"

"It seems more than fair."

She wanted to tell him how lovely and accommodating he had been through this entire relationship. But he already knew it, because she said it all the time. She knew that it appeared that she chose work over him the majority of the time; if she was honest with herself, that was exactly what she had done. But now they had a baby and the future all but beckoned a marriage. This was her life now, her new life, and she finally had a chance to not let work control it all. She'd done that once before and it had nearly caused a rift between her and Melissa.

She knew right away that something had changed. In the past, she would have wasted no time—she'd leave the table right away and start packing for the trip down to North Carolina tomorrow. But now, following the meeting with Duran and the conversation with Allen, all she wanted to do was sit there with him. He was her future, not her work. Allen, Michael, and Melissa could be the center of her life and that would be just fine.

All she had to do was make sure her heart was centered. To make sure she was able to settle in on a life that seemed so perfect.

And for now, sitting there with Allen, it seemed pretty damn perfect indeed.

Chapter Four

When Kate and DeMarco met up at the car in the bureau lot, it felt like they had not missed a beat. Still, there was something noticeably different about DeMarco that came down to more than just her appearance, which was pretty much the same as it had been since they'd last seen one another nearly six months ago.

"Agent Wise, it's nice to see you again," DeMarco said.

"Likewise."

They hugged briefly, and that was when, in something as simple as that quick show of affection, Kate could tell that there was something different about DeMarco. It had been less than eleven months since they had last worked together, but the woman had changed in ways that weren't easily identifiable. It was more than just the time apart and the way Duran had made her seem during their meeting. DeMarco looked different, too. Kate's first thought was that she looked older, but that wasn't quite right. She had the look of someone who held her head high, looking upward and forward without the need for someone else to hold her up. In that sense, yes, DeMarco appeared to be older. Having just had a baby, Kate finally figured out a fitting analogy: DeMarco's shift in appearance had gone from the naïve woman who wants to be a mother to the woman who had just had a baby, had become a mother, and was being guided by maternal instinct.

Another noticeable thing that had changed was the connection between Kate and DeMarco. It was noticeable from the very start—from the moment they tossed their bags into the trunk of the bureau sedan to start the drive to North Carolina. It was nothing negative. They were both ecstatic to see one another again, perhaps even more excited to be working a case again after nearly six months. But there was a sense of leadership change. DeMarco was no longer the subordinate, looking up to Kate and following her every lead. Now there was more confidence in DeMarco. She was an up and coming agent, cracking cases on her own.

Nothing was said—not from DeMarco nor from Duran—but Kate knew even before they were out of DC that DeMarco was the lead on this case. It was an intangible thing that Kate felt. And truth be told, she didn't care. It actually felt sort of *right.*

Most of the trip down was spent playing catch-up. There were six hours to do it and it went by far too fast. Kate shared stories about Michael and how it felt to have a newborn younger than her granddaughter. She talked about trying to stay active and to keep a sharp mind away from work when her world had been essentially making formula, changing diapers, and getting every bit of available sleep she could.

DeMarco, in turn, told her about her life. She kept the personal details to a minimum, giving only the bare essentials about a new woman she was dating and a cancer scare her father had lived through. But it was mostly about work. When she started discussing some of the highlights, she did so in an almost embarrassed way.

"There's no need to be timid about it," Kate said. "Duran told me how well you've been doing, particularly over the past several weeks. Now... when he said you *single-handedly* brought that killer in, what exactly did he mean?"

"You really want to hear about that?" She sounded surprised but, deep down, a little excited.

"Of course I do!"

"Well, I don't want to sound like I'm bragging. But yeah... this guy had killed a married couple in upstate New York and then attempted to kill and rob someone in DC. We found out he was here and a manhunt ensued. I wasn't the lead initially, but the lead came down with the flu and I was sort of forced into the role. I ended up cornering the killer and one of his friends in this old house just outside of Georgetown. I had to shoot the friend. Took out his left knee. Took the killer down in a pretty quick wrestling match. I accidentally dislocated his hip and fractured his wrist."

"*Accidentally* dislocated his hip?" Kate asked with a laugh.

"Yes, accidentally. Besides... he was high. Found out later that he was coming down off of some sort of psychedelic. Had he been of sound mind and knew what was going on, it might have ended very differently."

"Still, that's incredible. Maybe it's just the newfound mom coming out in me, but I'm proud of you."

"What's this *newfound* crap? Bitch, you're the Miracle Mom!"

They both laughed hard at this, setting the tone for the remainder of the trip. By the time they arrived in the small town of Harper Hills, it was almost as if they had not missed a beat. But still, that sense of a power shift was unmistakable. Kate accepted it warmly as DeMarco pulled their car into the police department parking lot, killed the engine, and eagerly opened the driver's side door.

⚜ ⚜ ⚜

The interior of the Harper Hills PD reminded Kate of what a police department from an '80s TV show might look like. And not one of those shows that took place in New York or LA. No, this place was just a step or two above Mayberry, something that might be featured in a Hallmark movie where the so-called detective was also a great cook or a children's book author. There was a central entry area that she supposed was the lobby. Beyond that, there were three desks, only one of which was occupied. Behind those desks was a thin hallway and nothing more.

The desk that was occupied was filled by an overweight gentleman with what Kate thought might be considered a mullet, adding to the '80s vibe. He nodded at them and got up from his seat quickly. The name tag on his left breast read **Smith.**

"You must be the agents," Smith said, hurrying to the lobby to greet them.

Kate took a step back, letting DeMarco know that she had the floor.

"That's us," DeMarco said. "Agents DeMarco and Wise. We were told we were to meet with Sheriff Gates."

"Yeah, that's right. He's back in his office." Smith waved them on to follow him. They did so, tailing him into the hall where he stopped at the first doorway on the right. "Sheriff?" he asked, knocking on the frame of the opened door. "The FBI agents are here."

"Come on in!" came the response.

DeMarco led the way, Kate following behind. The sheriff got to his feet and extended his hand to greet them. Kate bit back a grin at the idea that she had seen the police department as a few steps above the station from Mayberry in *The Andy Griffith Show.* Sheriff Gates actually looked like a younger, modernized version of Sheriff Andy from the titular show. He shook their hands and looked them in the eye in a way that told her he was perfectly fine working with women, but that he was also likely going to be treating them with some good old southern hospitality.

"Sheriff," Kate said, "I figured the station would be jumping, given the nature of this case."

"Well, it was a while ago. The State PD came in and I had two of my men go out with them. They're canvassing some of the back roads; there's a lot of them around here, you know. I stayed behind because I wanted to meet with you."

"We appreciate that," DeMarco said. "What exactly can you tell us about the case? We've been briefed in DC, of course, but I'd prefer to hear it straight from the source."

"Well, there's been two murders in a town that has only boasted a single homicide in the last ten years. Both have been young women—ages nineteen and twenty. The first victim was killed five nights ago, in a bowling alley parking lot. The other was found yesterday morning on the front porch of her mother's house. There's no clear link between the girls other than their age and that they were both locals. The latest victim, Kayla Peterson, was home from college for a few days."

"An in-state college?" DeMarco asked.

"No, somewhere down in Florida."

"Any links at all in the families of the women?" Kate asked.

"The only thing similar between them is that they both came from families of divorce. But we've spoken to all of the immediate family and everything seems to check out in terms of alibis. You, of course, are welcome to retread where we've already stepped."

"Thank you," DeMarco said. "Do you mind taking us out to the location where the second victim was found?"

"Yeah, absolutely."

Gates slipped on a jacket and exited the office ahead of them. Kate noticed how DeMarco seemed to carry herself differently now. It was a very slight difference, and not anything Kate could actually name, but it was there. She was more confident, more self-assured. It was present in the way she had interacted with the sheriff, even in that brief amount of time. It was also in the way she followed him but also led Kate.

She's still so young, Kate thought. *She's going to end up being an exceptional agent.*

It warmed her heart and made her incredibly glad to be back by DeMarco's side. More than anything though, it made her happy to be on this case, even though she was now quite sure it would be one of her last.

⚜ ⚜ ⚜

On the way to the latest murder scene, they passed through most of Harper Hills. There were four stoplights in the town and the most recognizable businesses were a Burger King and a Subway, both situated along the very short and mostly non-eventful Main Street. Near the end of Main Street, Gates turned his patrol car onto a back road, and DeMarco followed closely behind in the bureau sedan.

The back road turned into another and that one into yet another. It was a peculiar area, though. Kate had seen many backwoods towns set up in a similar way, but Harper Hills was almost like a rural subdivision without all the fringe, tucked away in the wooded flatlands of North Carolina. The neighborhood Gates led them into was not so much a neighborhood as a collection of wooded lots separated by thick groves of trees.

Kate leaned forward in her seat as Gates turned into a gravel driveway. DeMarco followed, both agents noticing that there was one other car in the driveway. She parked behind Gates and the three of them met one another at the start of the sidewalk.

"This is the Peterson residence," Gates said. "The mother, Sandra, is currently staying with an old family friend out near Cape Fear. She just couldn't stand to be around here. I get that, I suppose. She was torn up about it all. Catatonic."

He then handed DeMarco a manila envelope. DeMarco took it, opened it, and looked inside. Kate peered over her shoulder and saw that it was the case files. They had received most of those files digitally in DC, but not all of them. She always made a point to look at the physical files even when she had the digital ones. Something about seeing the information in print—especially crime scene photos—made the case seem more pressing.

"Were you the first on the scene?" DeMarco asked.

"No, that was Smith. But I was right behind him."

"Can you walk me through what you saw?"

Kate liked this approach. Rather than instantly looking though the offered files. DeMarco wanted to make sure she was seeing the scene as it had played out on the morning the body had been found. Photographs and notes were excellent tools, but rarely as good as hearing the events told from the mouths of those first on the scene.

"According to the mother, Kayla Peterson was home for a friend's wedding. She went out with some friends two nights ago and the next morning, she wasn't in her room. But her car was right there in the driveway. When the mother opened the door to check the car, she found Kayla dead on the porch. She'd gotten so far as putting her front door key into the lock before the killer attacked; they were still hanging from the knob when Smith and I got here. From the moment I saw the body, it was quite apparent she had been strangled."

"Was she fully clothed?" Kate asked.

"She was. The medical examiner said there was no indication that she had been raped or otherwise sexually assaulted. Seems like murder was the only thing the killer was interested in. Same goes for the first victim."

"Did the ME have any hints at what was used to strangle her?" DeMarco asked.

"He thinks some sort of cord, likely made of plastic. And the force with which he did it was a lot. The ME thinks the killer must be rather strong."

"Is that Kayla's car down there?" DeMarco asked, nodding to the only other car in the driveway.

"It is." He fished around in his pocket and took out a key fob that had been marked with an evidence tag. He handed it over to DeMarco and said, "Help yourself."

The three of them trotted back down the porch stairs to the driveway. Kayla had driven a 2017 Kia Optima. It looked exactly what Kate would expect a college girl's car to look like: fairly clean, the console littered with Chapstick, a half-empty plastic bottle of water, and a phone charger. Other than that, there was nothing of note in the car—certainly nothing that would help them determine who had been following her that night.

Following the car, Gates unlocked the front door. He explained to them that when Sandra Peterson had left town, she'd given Gates the keys to her home to help with the investigation.

"Any chance she'd be a suspect?" Kate asked.

"Even if I had the slightest inkling that she was—and I don't—it would not explain the first victim."

"That was three days before Kayla, right?" DeMarco asked.

"That's exactly right. While there is certainly no way to rule her out for certain, I interviewed every single person that was at the bowling alley when it closed up. Not a single person reported seeing Sandra Peterson. One woman knew exactly who I was talking about and thought it was outrageous that I was even asking. Besides . . . I go back to what the ME said. Whoever strangled Kayla Peterson was incredibly strong. And if you ever end up meeting Sandra Peterson, you'd have a hard time lining that up. She'd quite waifish. Lost a ton of weight when her husband left. And not by going to the gym. She looks almost malnourished. Sickly, at times."

Kate and DeMarco looked around the room Kayla had been staying in. It showed signs of the girl she once was, the residue of Hannah Montana stickers on the side of a dresser, faintly faded squares on the walls where posters once hung. They found two packed bags sitting at the foot of the bed. One had clearly been designated as the bag for all things related to the wedding celebration. It was filled with nicer clothes, makeup, and what looked like notes for a toast. The other bag was much less formal, with several outfits tossed in along with a paperback book and some toiletries. But there was nothing at all to help them with the case.

"Have you talked to any of the friends she was out with the night she was killed?" DeMarco asked.

"All but one of them. From what I gathered, there were four of them in all, including Kayla."

"I'd like to speak with all of them," DeMarco said. She then looked back to Kate, as if seeking approval. Kate only gave a quick nod of the head, appreciating the gesture of having DeMarco seek her opinion.

"Well, it's Monday afternoon, and they're all working. I could make some calls and see what I can do to get them all together. Maybe at the station."

"What about a bar or diner or something?" DeMarco asked.

Gates looked baffled, but nodded slowly. "Yeah, there's a bar or two in town. Well, right outside of it, actually. Pretty sure a few of the girls frequent one of them, a place called Esther's Place. I can have them meet you there at six or so."

"Make sure they know it's not optional," DeMarco said. "If they can't make it, we'll come to their house."

Kate smiled. It wasn't the path she would have taken, but it was an effective one. She knew what DeMarco was thinking. Typically, when the questioning of witnesses was done outside of interrogation rooms or even homes, the flow of conversation tended to be more natural. Kate had never preferred this approach, as the possibility of distraction became an issue. But this was DeMarco's show and she was going to let DeMarco run it her way.

The trio exited the house and by the time they reached their respective cars, Sheriff Gates was already on the phone, trying to organize the meeting.

"I wonder why he just let the mom leave like that," DeMarco said as they got into their car.

"The woman just lost her daughter. Unless there is substantial evidence that she is guilty or knows something worthwhile, there's no point in dragging her through this. Plus, the case files said she has no family or friends around here. And family and friends is exactly what she needs right now."

DeMarco chuckled. "Damn, I missed you, Kate. I was beginning to worry I put people's emotions in the back seat when it came to a case."

"It's easy to do," Kate said. "After a while, as sad as it sounds, it can become easy to stop seeing the people we meet on the cases as actual people. We just have a puzzle to solve and they are the tools to help. It's a shitty way to think, but I think all agents slip into it at some point or another."

"I can't see you behaving like that."

Talk to Melissa, she thought. *She'll tell you all about how I put the job above everything.*

The thought brought a sudden sting of tears to her eyes, which she wiped away. It was one more tug from life, pulling her closer. Yes, she had been a miserable mother to Melissa, usually choosing work over her.

She found herself back there again, only now twenty years later and with Michael. She had a chance to get it right this time.

And as that last thought still stung at her mind, she thought, when it was all said and done, she *would* get it right.

Chapter Five

The bar wasn't really a bar at all, but a drinking area within a greasy-spoon sort of diner. There were dartboards and even a by-God jukebox, but the diner section seemed to be why the establishment was there at all. The bar area within Esther's Place was pushed to the back, as if the owner might be ashamed of what took place there. But when Kate and DeMarco stepped inside at 5:45 to meet with the friends of Kayla Peterson, it seemed like a nice enough—if not slightly outdated—place.

There were three young women sitting at a booth in the far corner. Kate noticed right away that none of them were drinking alcohol, presumably because they were all under twenty-one. Two had waters, and another had what looked to be either seltzer water or Sprite. All three of them seemed to notice the FBI agents at the same time. They didn't look scared per se, but certainly on edge. Kate wondered how long the girls would wait until after the interview before they went out in search of a drink or two by illegal means.

DeMarco took the lead as they approached the table. "Are you ladies Claire Lee, Tabby Amos, and Olivia Macintyre?"

"That's us," the girl in the middle said. She had gorgeous red hair and a tall slender figure that came into view when she stood up and offered her hand. "I'm Tabitha Amos," she said. "Tabby to most, though."

"I'm Claire Lee," the girl on the left said. She was also quite pretty, but in a plain sort of way. She was wearing a thin hoodie and looked comfortable in it; she was clearly not the type that felt the need to look spectacular every time she left the house.

"And that makes me Olivia Macintyre," the last girl said. She had dark blonde hair that looked almost brown in the dim bar lighting. She wore a pair of stylish eyeglasses and had a mousy look about her.

"We're Agents DeMarco and Wise," DeMarco said. She showed her badge discreetly as she approached the table. "Mind if we join you?"

The trio of girls scooted closer together to allow room for Kate and DeMarco to sit at the booth. The moment they sat down, a waitress came over to take their orders. They both ordered waters and, having missed lunch, also a cheeseburger each to go. The girls seemed a little off put by this and Kate could see right away that DeMarco's decision to meet them here had been a smart one.

"So, as I'm sure Sheriff Gates told you," Demarco said, "we want to talk about Kayla Peterson. We especially need to know anything you can tell us about that last night you all spent together."

The girls looked at one another somberly. They all looked upset about current events but mostly well-centered. Kate wasn't too surprised to find that Tabby Amos was the mouthpiece for the group. Most people would view her as the prettiest, and therefore the most outwardly confident, of the group. She had also been the first to stand and introduce herself.

"Well, it was my idea. The four of us were very tight in high school. Then Kayla and Claire over there decided to go to college and we rarely saw one another. We all got together last Christmas . . . that was the last time the four of us were together. I thought it would be cool to have one last hurrah before the wedding."

"When *is* the wedding?" Kate asked.

"This coming Saturday," Olivia said.

"Who's getting married?"

"My brother," Olivia said.

"He was sort of a big brother to all of us when we were in high school," Tabby said. "Had rough words with some of the creeps that asked us out and couldn't handle the rejection."

"I'm one of the maids of honor," Olivia said. "And I invited all of my friends, of course."

"But we figure it would be stupid to have a rip-roaring night of fun the day before the wedding," Tabby said. "So we decided to do it Saturday night."

"What did you all do?" DeMarco asked.

"Hung out at my house for a while," Claire said. "Well, I suppose it's my parents' house. But they were away for the weekend, knew I was in town and wanted to hang out with my friends. So they were cool with everyone coming over. We watched some movies, drank some wine, ate some pizza."

"Did you go anywhere else at all?"

"Kayla and I went out to the supermarket in Glensville to get more wine," Olivia said.

"Where is Glensville?"

"About twenty minutes away from Harper Hills."

"You couldn't just get wine somewhere in town?" Kate asked.

"No," Tabby said. "We're all under twenty-one and everyone knows everyone else in this town."

"Yeah," Olivia said. "Plus, there's this guy in Glensville that I used to date, a few years older than me. He knows the manager at the supermarket in Glensville. They didn't card and let us get some drinks." She paused here and then added: "Shit. They aren't going to get into trouble, are they?"

"They should," DeMarco said. "But that's smalltime compared to what we're dealing with right now. Now... did anything of note happen in Glensville?"

"Nothing," Olivia said. "We went in, got three bottles of wine, and left."

"Any cross words with this guy you used to date?"

"No. Hell, I barely even spoke to him. He had his new girlfriend with him anyway. He was sort of in a rush to get out of there."

"Did anyone end up drinking too much that night?" Kate asked.

"All four of us," Tabby said. "I was sort of pissed when I found out Kayla had left. Her mom's house is only like ten minutes from Claire's house, but still. It was irresponsible of her to drink and drive. Of course, then I found out she had been killed and..."

"What do you mean *when you found out Kayla had left*?" DeMarco asked.

"Well, near midnight Claire brought out some of her folks' liquor," Tabby said. "We had a little too much to drink. I faded out sometime around one."

"I blinked out shortly after that," Claire said.

"Yeah," Olivia added. "Kayla and I were the last ones hanging in there. I don't think she drank any of the liquor. Sure, she was sort of buzzed, but I don't think she was flat out drunk. Not when I passed out, anyway."

"So you all think she just saw that everyone had passed out and decided to go home?" DeMarco asked.

"Seemed that way," Claire said.

"And she didn't call or text any of you when she left?" Kate asked. "She didn't leave a note or anything?"

"Nothing," Olivia said.

"I just assumed she was a little embarrassed," Tabby said. "She was never a huge drinker in the first place. I don't think that changed when she went to college. Of course, maybe she was just embarrassed to be hanging out with a few friends that never decided to get out of Harper Hills and go to college. I don't know."

"Was she acting any different than you can remember her acting in the past?" Kate asked.

"No, and that's the weirdest thing of all," Claire said. "She was the same old Kayla. Cracking jokes, open, honest. It was almost like nothing at all had changed since we'd graduated high school."

DeMarco asked a few more questions, specifically about the conversation they could remember having the night Kayla had died. While she orchestrated the question, Kate did her best to size up the demeanor and body language of the three girls. She had no reason to suspect that any of them would be hiding something, but her attention did keep coming back to Olivia. She was fidgeting slightly and her eyes would not stay in one place for very long.

She's the only one that was alone with Kayla on the night she died, Kate thought. *Maybe we could get more out of her if the other two weren't here.* She made a mental note and filed it away as DeMarco wrapped up the last of her questions.

The waitress brought their burgers and the agents gave their farewells. DeMarco ended the conversation by giving each of the girls one of her business cards, instructing them to call her if they thought of anything else or heard any murmurs about what had happened to Kayla.

"What do you think?" DeMarco asked Kate as they walked back out to their car.

"I think Olivia may have had more to say if her friends hadn't been around. She seemed antsy. And she was the only one that spent any alone time with Kayla."

"You think something happened when they went out for that extra wine?"

"I don't know. But even if not, I wonder if they maybe talked about something that might have been related to what happened later. It's all speculation, but..."

"No, I saw that she was sort of uneasy, too."

They both considered this as they got into the car. Night was slowly falling and though the day felt long, Kate knew it was not over yet. DeMarco had always been a night owl, milking every last minute and ounce of productivity out of the day.

And that was fine with Kate. Because as the first day of the case came toward a close, something in her heart became more and more certain that this may be her last case. If that were true, she intended to make the most of it.

Chapter Six

DeMarco was doing everything she could to not overthink things. But she also had to be honest with herself. For a moment, as brief as it may have been, she had been a little pissed off when Duran informed her Kate would be joining her for this case. That disappointment had quickly been replaced by joy, though. Her partnership with Kate Wise had been, at first, almost like a mentorship. But as they had grown and learned each other's habits and mannerisms, it had become something more. Still, along the way, DeMarco had always felt that she had been a junior agent . . . someone still learning the ropes, hoping to impress Kate as her own skillset continued to develop and mature.

DeMarco knew this case was hers. Kate had come on board at the last minute and was going out of her way to remain in the back seat. While DeMarco appreciated the gesture more than she could express, it was making her feel uncomfortable. Kate was a born leader and something about watching her knowingly give up control was odd.

It also made DeMarco wonder what might be going on behind the scenes. How was Kate viewing her career now that she was the so-called Miracle Mom and had finally come back to work?

DeMarco wasn't sure, but had a feeling she'd know by the time this case came to a close. First, of course, they had to close it.

She pulled into Larry's Lanes and Arcade at 6:15. The parking lot was mostly empty, colored a strange red in the faded neon of the word ARCADE in the sign out front. DeMarco parked as close to the front as she could, not sure where the body of the first victim had been found. As she and Kate walked inside, DeMarco paged through the contents of the case reports, having filed them to memory last night before going to sleep.

The victim was Mariah Ogden, nineteen years of age. She had been found by the owner of Larry's Lanes and Arcade at 10:40 on Wednesday night. She had been lying on the pavement behind her car. Though Larry had not seen them, the coroner's report detailed the bruising around her neck and the evidence of immense pressure against her windpipe. Mariah, like Kayla, had been strangled by someone who appeared to be quite strong. So far, it seemed no one had seen what had happened and there were no leads at all.

DeMarco and Kate approached the shoe rental counter, where a man of sixty or so was standing by a small television. He looked extremely bored. A quick glance of the fifteen lanes behind her revealed that only two lanes were occupied—one by five middle-aged women and another, all the way at the far end of the building, by a lone man.

The man behind the shoe rental counter nodded to them as they approached, giving them a strange look. The lapel on his shirt read LARRY. "Can I help you?"

DeMarco acted quickly before there could be any odd tension between her and Kate. She showed her badge and ID and said, "Agents DeMarco and Wise, with the FBI. I was hoping to get some information about the death of Mariah Ogden."

"I already told the cops everything I know," Larry said. "But if it'll help find who's been killing these girls, I don't mind."

"You said girls," Kate said. "As in more than one. I assume you heard about the second victim?"

"Can't help but hear terrible news like that pretty quickly in a town as small as this one. Yeah… it was Kayla Peterson, right? Home for a wedding, from what I hear."

"Larry, how did you find Mariah's body?" DeMarco asked.

"I had closed the place down. Walked out to my truck and saw a car still in the parking lot, all the way over near the edge. Sometimes the teenagers hang out over there after they've bowled. So I walked over to see what was going on. Figured maybe just someone left their car there while going out somewhere else with a friend. But as I got closer to it, I saw a sneaker. And then I saw a leg attached to it. And there was Mariah Ogden, right behind her car."

"Already dead?"

"Yeah. But I don't think for very long. I heard there was bruising on her throat. But I didn't see any when I found her like that."

"Had she been in here that night?"

"Not that night, no. But she would come in here from time to time with her friends."

He was about to say something else, but was interrupted by the clatter of pins falling and cheering from the crowd of middle-aged ladies. When the noise quieted down, Larry continued.

"She was a lovely girl, really. Very polite, well-mannered."

"Do you know anyone in the crowd she typically hung around with?" DeMarco asked.

"Not really well, no. But you may want to check with him." He nodded behind him, in the direction of the man who was bowing by himself.

"Who's that?"

"His name is Dwayne Patterson. He would sometimes be with the crowds Mariah would come in with. Bashful kid. He's here a lot, sometimes by himself, but usually sort of meanders from crowd to crowd. I have no real evidence to support this, but the way he sometimes looked at Mariah and laughed at anything she said... I think he might have fancied her a bit."

"Thank you, Larry," Kate said.

He gave a wink to them both as they turned and headed for the lane all the way to the left. As they approached, Dwayne Patterson rolled a ball that left him with a dreaded 7-10 split. He angled his head as if hoping to see something different and then approached the ball return machine. As he waited for his ball, he spotted DeMarco and Kate. There was no mistaking where they were headed; he knew they were coming to speak to him and it showed in his eyes. He looked like a trapped cat, cornered by two feral dogs.

"Mr. Patterson," DeMarco said as they approached the ball machine. "Larry over there says you might be a good resource for information about Mariah Ogden."

It was clear that Patterson had not yet decided if he should be fearful or not. He eyed them skeptically and asked: "And just who the hell are you?"

This time, DeMarco and Kate moved at the same time, showing their IDs in tandem like a well-rehearsed magic trick. "Agents DeMarco and Wise, FBI. Now, do you want to be just a bit more accommodating?"

Slowly, Patterson took a seat behind the scorekeeping machine. "Sorry. I had no idea. Um . . . yeah, I mean, I knew her. Not super great or anything, but I knew her."

"How old are you, Mr. Patterson?" Kate asked.

"Nineteen."

"Would you say you and Mariah were friends?"

"Sure. We were friends through most of school, just not best friends, you know?"

"Sure," Kate said. "How about this past Wednesday night? Did you see her then?"

"Yeah, that was the night she died. I was here, bowling with a friend. When he and I left, I saw that Mariah and a few of her friends were hanging out in the parking lot."

"Is that something she did a lot?"

"Not a lot, no. But from time to time. There's not really much else to do around here, you know?"

DeMarco did know. She'd grown up in a similar town where the only thing to do after hours was hang out in convenience store parking lots, smoking cigarettes and maybe making out when the coast was clear.

"Did you go over to hang out?" DeMarco asked.

"Just for a little while. At first, I mean. I took my friend home and then swung back by just to check in."

"Check in on what, exactly?" Kate asked.

Patterson frowned, sensing that he might be venturing into dangerous territory. Slowly, he started to do his best to explain. There were nerves in his voice, as well as something else. Regret, maybe? DeMarco wasn't sure.

"Well, she was hanging out with some of the regulars . . . some friends of hers from high school and a new girl she met at the community college in Charlotte. But there was this other guy with them, some dude I've seen a few times and just . . . I don't know . . . sort of avoided. I went back by later to check on Mariah to see if he was still around."

"Why would you avoid this guy?" DeMarco asked.

"He's sort of creepy, you know? The type that used to hang around the high school parking lot a few years after he had already graduated. He's got to be at least twenty-five."

"And what were the ages of the crowd you and Mariah hang out with?"

"Between nineteen and twenty-one or so. I hate to stereotype someone like that, but he's sort of a loser. But anyway . . . that night, it was clear that he was drunk. Being loud and belligerent, you know?"

"What's this guy's name?" Kate asked.

"Does anyone need to know I was the one that told you?"

"Absolutely not."

"Jamie Griles." There was some grit and anger in his voice as he said it. "There's no hard proof, but a lot of people think he goes to high school parties to get girls drunk and then sleeps with them. So when I saw that he was hanging out with Mariah and those younger girls, it felt creepy."

"And was he still here in the parking lot when you came back by?"

"No, he had already left. One of Mariah's friends said there was a party somewhere and even joked that Jamie went because there were younger girls there."

"Is Jamie Griles a local?" DeMarco asked.

"Yeah. Born and raised. He'll die here, too. Loser won't ever amount to anything." Patterson chuckled and shook his head. "Says the nineteen-year-old mechanic bowling by himself on a Monday night."

"Have you spoken to the police?"

"No. No one bothered talking to me. Like I said . . . I wasn't best friends with her. Just . . . a guy that knew her."

The way he said this made DeMarco think Larry had been right; Dwayne Patterson had feelings for Mariah Ogden. She wondered if he ever told Mariah. The way he was handling it made her think he had not—that he had kept his feelings bottled up.

"Did you not think to talk to them about Jamie Griles?" Kate asked.

"Well, I didn't even pause to think he might have been the one to kill her. Yeah, the guy is a creep and a loser, but I don't know that I'd put murder within his reach."

"You said he was loud and belligerent," DeMarco said. "Do you know if there was anyone in particular he was upset with?"

"No clue."

DeMarco looked around the bowling alley, as if searching for more questions to ask. When it was clear that they were done, she handed out yet another one of her business cards. "Please don't hesitate to call if you think of anything else or even hear about anything that might be about Mariah's murder."

"I will," Patterson said, pocketing the card. "Thanks."

The *thanks* seemed a little odd, but DeMarco could tell by the resigned look on the young man's face that he was happy to have helped, even if only in the slightest of ways. He was already picking up his ball to try managing that 7-10 split when DeMarco and Kate turned and walked away.

Chapter Seven

"You think it's too late to make a house call?" DeMarco asked.

Kate laughed as she buckled her seatbelt. As soon as Dwayne Patterson had given them Jamie Griles's name, she knew they would be making at least one more stop before calling it a day. She envied the drive and energy DeMarco had and could clearly see why she was so quickly making a name for herself in the bureau.

"Not for someone with the lifestyle that Jamie Griles seems to lead," Kate said. "I assume that's the stop you'd like to make?"

"Figured it might be worth a shot. It's not even seven o'clock yet."

"I'll call Gates and see if he can pull up an address."

Kate placed the call to Gates, only to find that he wasn't at the precinct. He patched her through to Smith's desk. The officer seemed happy enough to help, coming up with an address within twenty seconds.

Just as Kate plugged the address into the map app on her phone, her hand started to buzz as Gates called her back.

"Can I ask what you're looking into Griles for?" Gates asked.

"We got word that he was hanging out with Mariah Ogden's group of friends on the night she was killed. He was apparently loud and possibly intoxicated."

"I should warn you that he's a creep of the highest degree. But I honestly don't see him as the sort to kill anyone."

"That's what we're hearing. Now, can you define *creep*?"

"I've arrested him at last three times in the past few years. Small stuff, mostly. He's got a DUI on his record, as well as a charge for disturbing the peace when he decided to start a little bar brawl at Esther's Place. And, as I'm sure you may have already heard, he has something of a habit of trying to impress younger girls... often by purchasing alcohol for them. We haven't been able to bust him for that yet, but it's pretty much common knowledge."

"Yeah, we're hearing all of that, too."

"Let me know if you need a hand."

Kate ended the call, starting to wonder if Griles might be more of a lead than she had originally thought. She checked the address in her GPS and saw that it was only sixteen minutes away from the Larry's Lanes and Arcade.

"You thinking the killer might be some sort of jilted or rejected ex-boyfriend or something?" Demarco asked as she guided them to the address.

"In a small town like this, it's where my mind automatically goes at first," Kate said. "But until we can accurately look at any links between the two girls, that's going to be hard to nail down. It's the one reason I really wish the mother was still here."

"Maybe we can call her tomorrow," DeMarco said. It was more of a question, though—a veiled way to ask: *Would we be total monsters if we bothered the grieving mother tomorrow?*

"If nothing pans out tonight, we may have to," Kate said.

"The thing that's hanging me up is *where* Kayla Peterson was killed. Right there on her front porch. I mean, she even got the key in the door. Makes me think she had the guy *with* her."

"Maybe trying to sneak him into her house?" Kate asked.

"Maybe."

"There's another possibility, too. Maybe he was there, waiting for her."

DeMarco nodded gravely. "Neither one of those scenarios is particularly pleasant."

As DeMarco drove to the address they had been given, Kate looked over the notes on the iPad DeMarco had been uploading all of the case files to. So far there wasn't much to look at, but there were small things to pick up on here and there.

"Both victims went to the same high school," Kate noted as she read through the notes. "Although in a town this small that's really not too much of a surprise."

"Different colleges," DeMarco pointed out. "Kayla Peterson went way off to Florida for college. Mariah Ogden went to Western View Community College, just outside of Charlotte."

"I would be curious to know if Jamie Griles knew Kayla. If so, that would basically be the only link between them."

"And that wouldn't be good news for Griles," DeMarco said, thinking it over.

It was the last thing either of them said, though Kate was pretty sure DeMarco was feeling the same stirrings of excitement she was. They were on their way to question their first concrete lead and that was always am exciting moment. Kate allowed herself to enjoy it, though as they drove through the night she could not ignore just how badly she was starting to miss Michael.

She felt the old stings of feeling like a bad mother, of leaving her family behind. It was more than the guilt of any mother who went back to work after maternity leave, though. No, these were stings from the past, stings she had suffered through and thought she had managed to put behind her.

But these stings... these were fresh. And they seemed to be reiterating the same cries of her heart. Maybe this *was* her last hoorah.

Maybe she shouldn't even be here at all.

⚜ ⚜ ⚜

They covered the rest of the trip to Jamie Griles's residence in silence. When they arrived, they found themselves pulling into a small gravel parking lot in front of what appeared to be a four-plex. It looked like one large house, divided into four different living spaces or apartments. Each apartment had its own mailbox at the mouth of the parking lot. Kate noted that the one marked 3 held the name J. GRILES.

DeMarco parked beside a beaten-up old GMC pickup, parked slightly crooked in front of the third apartment. As they got out, Kate heard the rumbling of a stereo coming from one of the apartments. She was rather proud to find she knew the song as "Battery" by Metallica. Melissa had gone through a Metallica phase in her youth and had been both surprised and humiliated to find that her mother hadn't outright hated the music.

As they approached the door with a bronze 3 in its center, she realized the music was not coming from inside. However, someone was home: a soft light filled the window, mostly blocked by lopsided blinds. As Kate stepped onto the stoop, DeMarco knocked.

"Yeah!" was the response from inside. "One minute!"

There was some brief commotion from inside and then, about twenty seconds after knocking, the door was opened. Jamie Griles was an average-sized man. His black hair was held up in a style that nearly reminded Kate of Elvis, held in place by stiff-looking product. He had small eyes and a chiseled jaw that was covered in five o'clock shadow. He wasn't handsome, but he was far from unattractive as well. It didn't take much effort for Kate to imagine impressionable young girls to give him some attention in exchange for beer or other things.

He smiled at the two women and said: "Can I help you ladies?"

DeMarco apparently took offense to the way he was looking at them. When she took out her ID and badge, she basically thrust them at him. "Agents DeMarco and Wise, FBI. Are you Jamie Griles?"

"I am," he said. The smile was gone, replaced by what appeared to be genuine confusion. "But... FBI? What for?"

"We're investigating a case here in Harper Hills and would like a word with you."

He looked back and forth between them, maybe trying to figure out if this was some sort of prank. When it was clear that he had no intention of inviting them in, Kate took a single step forward. "Mr. Griles, can we come inside?"

"I mean... yeah, sure, but... what for?"

Kate noticed that DeMarco took him up on the invitation before explaining the purpose of the visit. It was a good move, as Griles would have surely become protective and defensive if he knew they were going to ask him about two recent murders in the area.

Kate followed DeMarco into a small and messy living room. The television against the far wall was tuned to a baseball game. There was a bottle of cheap whiskey on the coffee table and a still-burning cigarette in an ashtray next to it.

DeMarco started right away, before Griles even had time to close his door. "Mr. Griles, do you have any idea why we might be here?"

"No," he said. He was clearly scared, but there was a growing irritation beneath it. He did not enjoy being questioned—to be made to feel as though he was less than. "And I don't think you should make me guess."

It was interesting for Kate to watch the back and forth, the cat and mouse. DeMarco had set a trap, and Griles had sidestepped it. Kate would have tried the exact same thing, though. The vague question from DeMarco had given

Griles the opportunity to confess to buying alcohol for minors—which was a very serious charge in the state of North Carolina. But Griles had dodged it and put the ball right back into DeMarco's court.

"Mr. Griles, it's a small town," DeMarco said. "Can I assume you've heard about the recent murders in the area?"

"I have. Word does get around."

"You know their names?" Kate asked.

"Yes," he said. He was being careful with the way he spoke. It was clear that this was not the first time he had been questioned by someone in authority. She could picture Griles and Sheriff Gates having this same sort of back and forth quite easily.

"Tell me, please," DeMarco said.

"Why? Are you here because you think I had something to do with it?"

"I said no such thing," DeMarco said. "But in investigating the murders, we discovered today that you were included in a small group of people who last saw one of the victims."

Griles nodded at this and actually seemed a little relieved. "You mean Mariah?"

"Yes. Mariah Ogden. We have a witness that saw you with her and a group of other underage kids outside of Larry's Lanes on the night she died. What do you say to that?"

"I say there are some nosy-ass people in this town."

"You make a habit of hanging out with younger girls, Mr. Griles?" Kate asked.

"Sometimes," he said. "But anything I do is consensual. I'm not one of those rapist assholes."

"Our witness says you were loud and a little off the hinge that night," DeMarco said. "Had something been bothering you?"

"No. And I don't recall being loud and out of control."

"Had you been drinking?"

"A bit, yes."

"We have it on good authority that you left that group and went somewhere else," Kate said. "Could you give us a timeline of events after you left the Larry's Lanes parking lot?"

"I can. And I have a few people that could back me up if…"

He paused here, sat down in a ratty old recliner, and looked at both women as if they had just hurt his feelings.

"Something wrong, Mr. Griles?" DeMarco asked.

"You *do* think I'm a suspect."

"An older man who is known for trying to impress younger girls just admitted to hanging out with a recent murder victim on the night she died," DeMarco said. "Yes. Any agent worth a damn would question you. So give us that timeline."

He plucked the cigarette from the ashtray, took a drag, and settled into the chair. "I left the bowling alley with a buddy of mine, Gary. We went to Esther's for a couple of drinks and some buffalo wings. After that, we went to a house party for a while."

"Where was this party?" Kate asked.

"I don't even know the guy. Some senior... his folks were away."

"Did your friend Gary go with you?"

"Yeah, Gary and another buddy of mine. The three of us went together. This other buddy, Sammy, he drove because he hadn't been drinking yet."

"How many people were at this party?" Kate asked.

"Not many, actually. I'd say no more than twenty or so."

"All high school kids?"

Griles gave her that same scolded-dog look and nodded. "Yeah, except me, Gary, and Sammy."

"Do you remember when you left the party?" DeMarco asked.

"No, not exactly. Probably around ten thirty or so. It was a lame party."

"How did you get home?"

A little grimace came to his face at this question. He looked at DeMarco out of the corner of his eye and sighed. "You really need to know that?"

"It would help. If we can tell where you were every moment between leaving that parking lot and ten forty-five, we can scratch your name off of the suspects list."

"I got a ride with a girl. She brought me home and she... well, she stayed over."

"A high school girl?"

"No, actually. She graduated last year. And yes, she's eighteen."

DeMarco frowned, as if she did not buy this at all. "So she brought you here, and you guys... had a sleepover. Would she give us the same story?"

"Yeah, she would. But really... do you need to call her?"

"It would go a long way in clearing your name."

Griles stubbed his cigarette out and reached for the liquor bottle. "We swore no one would ever know. She's not exactly a catch."

"And you are?" DeMarco said.

Kate bit back a smile. She had been thinking the exact same thing but would have kept it quiet.

Griles said nothing in response. He took a swig from the whiskey bottle and then dug his cell phone out of his pocket. For the next two minutes, Griles gave DeMarco the numbers of the two friends who accompanied him to the party, as well as the number of the apparently reluctant sleepover date, a young woman named Charlene Hooper.

"And what about Saturday night, early Sunday morning?" Kate asked. "Have any witnesses as to where you were?"

He grinned, though there was no humor or light-heartedness to it. "That's Kayla Peterson, right? I hear she got killed, too."

"That's correct. We don't know when, exactly, but it would have been sometime between one thirty and seven or so in the morning."

He shrugged. "I was out and about until about midnight. Then I was back here, playing some drinking games with Sammy and Gary."

"For how long?"

"About two or so, I'd say."

"Can anyone back this up?"

"Sammy and his girl, I suppose. They crashed on the couch, over there."

Kate and DeMarco looked to one another and gave quick nods of approval. The stories would be easy enough to check out. DeMarco started to head for the door, Kate taking the lead.

"Thanks for your time, Mr. Griles."

"Yeah," he said. Then, as an afterthought, he added: "I never really knew Mariah, just so you know. I tried hooking up with her a few times, but she was too good, you know? For real... I don't know anything about what happened to her. I hope you find who did it."

Kate watched as DeMarco gave him an uncertain glance. "I appreciate that."

With that, the agent stepped out of the pungent smell of cigarette smoke and into the fresh night air. The evening was cold, promising a pretty chill night, but it was nice to be out of all of the smoke.

When they left his apartment, Griles watched them go. Kate had seen the look on his face a million times before. He did not trust them. And oddly enough, that usually meant the suspect was not guilty. It was often strange how that all worked out.

"What do you think?" DeMarco asked.

"I think Gates was right when he referred to the guy as a creep. But I also think once we call all these numbers, we're going to find out he's telling the truth."

Demarco pulled out of the parking lot and back out onto the road. "Let's get to calling them, then," she said. "I'd rather get in touch with them before Griles does."

Chapter Eight

Sammy—full name Sammy Curtis—did not answer his phone. It went straight to voicemail, and Kate did not leave a message. She then called Gary—full name Gary Hamilton—while DeMarco drove back down Harper Hills' Main Street. Night had fallen, and the little rotating digital clock outside of the BB&T bank on Main Street read 8:11. As the time spun away from Kate, a gruff male voice with a thick southern accent answered the phone. The accent was so present that it was noticeable in the simple one-word greeting.

"Hello?"

"Am I speaking with Mr. Gary Hamilton?"

"You are. Who's this?"

Kate told him and Gary Hamilton was surprisingly accommodating. He gave them the address to his home and even apologized beforehand for the miserable shape it was in. The address he gave them was six miles away from where Jamie Griles lived. Gary lived in a simple little house, tucked away down a driveway that was about a quarter of a mile long, and hidden by the strip of woodland that separated it from the road.

The porch light was on when they arrived, and the door was answered less than ten seconds after DeMarco knocked. The man who answered the door was slightly cleaner-looking than Jamie Griles. He had a close-cropped haircut and had the sort of facial features that would make him look thirty in some lights, and twenty in others. Kate guessed him to be around twenty-one or twenty-two.

"Come on in," he said. "Can I get you anything to drink?"

"No thank you," DeMarco said. "Mr. Hamilton, as my partner told you on the phone, we're agents DeMarco and Wise with the FBI. We're trying to uncover some answers about two recent murders in the area and need you to confirm the whereabouts of Jamie Griles this past Saturday night and last Wednesday night."

"Yeah, I can do that, sure."

As they went through the back and forth of it with him, recounting all that Jamie Griles had told them and having Gary back it all up, Kate noticed that Gary did not look nervous or scared at all. If anything, he looked very interested—almost excited. Kate figured he was the good ol' boy type, the local that wanted to do whatever he could to bring a killer to justice in his small town.

It took less than three minutes for Gary to confirm every single bit of Jamie's story. He even chuckled a bit when he learned that Jamie had given Charlene Hooper's name.

"Yeah, Jamie is a handful, all right," Gary said. "He's got a bd reputation for his penchant for younger girls—and he *should.* But honestly, he's a good dude at heart, you know? He'd give you the shirt off his back."

"What about this other guy?" Kate asked. "Sammy Curtis. You feel the same way about him?"

"No. I mean, I don't *dislike* him, but he'd sort of a jerk. Always making sure he lets people know what he thinks of them, but in this really shitty passive-aggressive way, you know? Always tries to make girls feel ugly, tries to make guys feel weak."

"But you're friends with him?" DeMarco asked.

"No. I'm friends with Jamie. Sammy just sort of pops up here and there to hang out. He hangs with Jamie because he knows Jamie tends to hang around a lot of younger girls. He also freeloads off of us. Beer, a place to crash, things like that."

"Is he a local?"

"Sort of. He's just a few miles outside of Harper Hills."

"Forgive us for asking, but you *were* with Griles and Curtis last Wednesday. So you check out for that. Can you tell us where *you* were Saturday night?"

"Oh yeah," he said, shaking his head. "I work for the town custodian. Sort of a repairman, jack of all trades deal. We got a call Saturday around seven thirty in the evening that there was a burst water pipe out on Fleetwood Road. It had a ditch flooding, running across the road and affected the water supply to damn near two hundred residential addresses. I was out with a crew until about one thirty in the morning cleaning that mess up."

"What about after one thirty?" Kate asked.

"I came back home. I did get a call from my supervisor just after two, asking questions. But that's about as late as I have proof of anything."

"Any idea what Sammy might have been up to Saturday night?"

"No clue. He might have been with Jamie, but I don't know for sure."

"Can you think of any time last Wednesday when Sammy was out of your sight? Between leaving Esther's Place and going to that party, or from the party to Jamie's house?"

"There were spots here and there, yeah. But I figured he was out getting beer or a girl or something. It's not unusual for Sammy to show up, sort of disappear for an hour or so, and then show up again. He's a strange dude."

"Any idea where he might be right now?" Kate asked.

"I don't know. Like I said… we're not exactly friends. I do, however, happen to know where he lives. Does that help?"

"That helps tremendously," DeMarco said, already taking her phone out to type in the address.

⚜ ⚜ ⚜

Kate did not consider herself a judgmental person, nor did she allow herself to resort to stereotypes. But the moment DeMarco pulled their car into Sammy Curtis's driveway, one single term came to mind before she could stop it: white trash.

The house was a ramshackle mess. The front porch was crooked, to the point of being partially collapsed. On the right side of its single story, an ancient air conditioning unit hung from a window, the back side mostly rusted. A broken down truck without any tires was up on blocks to the right side of the property—a property that looked as if it had not seen a mower in a good while. Ironically, there was a very nice-looking truck parked in what served as the driveway. It was an older model Dodge Ram but had been modified and well taken care of. It was polarizing, sure, but was also one of the things Kate had come to expect from people who lived in impoverished areas in America—particularly in the south. They'd prefer to spend money on vehicles or new technology as a means to show their fabricated success rather than take care of their homes and other property.

They got out of the car and started toward the house. Kate hesitated by the truck, though. If this truck was his pride and joy, what sort of things might he keep in it? She stepped over to the driver's side and thought for a moment. It was older—probably around a 2011 or 2012 model—so there would be no alarm if she tried opening the door. She reached out, tried the handle, and found it unlocked. The dome light came on, glowing weakly onto her.

"What are you doing?" DeMarco asked.

"Just having a look."

"Maybe we should talk to him first," DeMarco said. She did not seem upset that Kate was crossing such a line; if anything, she sounded surprised and a little alarmed.

"Might be good to have some insider info before we talk to him... especially if he's the type of person Gary Hamilton described him as being."

DeMarco said nothing, but she did hurry over to where Kate was currently leaning into the truck. She found a tool bag resting in the floorboard, pressed against the console between the driver's and passenger's seat. She was well aware that she should not be doing something like this without a warrant, but she was surprisingly not bothered by it. She reached to the bag and pulled it to her. It was quite heavy, and several tools rattled and clanked against one another. She opened it up and looked inside. All she found were two hammers, a level, a wrench, and an assortment of well-used screwdrivers.

Feeling a little embarrassed to have been snooping, she shoved the bag back where it came from. She then checked under the driver's seat. There was a small 9mm in a holster, but this wasn't of any real concern. There were a huge number of people in this part of the state with permits to carry weapons.

"Hey, Wise?" DeMarco's voice, soft and a little worried sounding, came from beside her. "You see that?"

Kate didn't at first. But then she saw that DeMarco was pointing to the thin space between the backs of the seats and the rear wall of the truck. It was littered with old cracker wrappers and other debris, but sitting on top of it all was a cord of some kind. It was purple, and looked like to be made of silk. It was curled up on itself, and was about the width of a basic piece of rope.

"Seems like a strange item to be hanging out in a man's truck, right?" DeMarco said.

Thinking of the strangulation marks around the necks of both of the victims, Kate only nodded. And then, without saying another word, they both started walking toward the decrepit house.

As it turned out, they didn't even have to knock. About three seconds after they stepped up onto the hazardous porch, the front door opened. First there was the creaking of the primary door, and then the scratching of a screen door being pushed open, the crooked frame grating against the porch.

A tall man stood in the door, slightly hunched over. Despite his height, he was exceptionally skinny. "You the FBI?" he asked.

"Good guess," DeMarco said, showing her badge. "Can we assume your buddy Jamie Griles gave you a heads-up?"

"Assume all you want." He crossed his arms and propped himself against the doorframe, letting them know that they would not be coming inside.

"Mr. Curtis, you're being quite confrontational," Kate said. "It's really unnecessary. We just want to ask you some questions."

"Questions about two dead women, right? You think I had something to do with it?"

Kate could see DeMarco retraining herself. She was getting much better at it. The only way Kate saw it was because she had been working with the woman off and on for a year and a half.

"Actually, we were just going to ask you to confirm the whereabouts of Jamie Griles last Wednesday night," DeMarco said. "But the way you're reacting to simply paying a visit does make me wonder if we need to go deeper with you."

"I'm not stupid," he said. "I know I don't have to answer your questions."

"That's right, you don't," Kate said. "But if you give us a hard time, we do have the right to just keep coming and coming. It might be us, it might Sheriff Gates. Some days it might be the State Police. And the more you refuse to talk, the more guilty you look. You understand that, right?"

His eyes flickered the briefest little bit. He was certainly hiding something. The discovery of the silk cord in the back of his truck suddenly started to sit heavy on Kate's mind.

"Well then, I guess you'll have to get used to coming out here, then," Sammy Curtis said. "I'm not putting up with two bitchy women asking me about two women being killed. I might be an asshole, but I'm no murderer."

"At least you're admitting to the former," DeMarco said.

"Well," Kate said, feeling the question coming and knowing she should stop it. She was venturing into dishonest territory—a place she had been before, but tried to avoid whenever possible. "If you won't answer our questions about the murders, maybe you'll tell us why you have a silk cord tucked behind the seat of your truck."

The glare he sent her way was just barely stronger than the one DeMarco gave her as she turned to look at her. Kate had just revealed that they had snooped in his truck. If Curtis was smart enough (and that was a big *if*), he could use it against them if he found himself in trouble.

"How the hell do you know about that?" he asked, looking out to his truck.

Kate thought quickly, surprised at how quickly the lie came to her. "There was a small portion of it hanging out of your door," she said. "Given some of the specific details about these cases, we had no choice but to investigate."

Curtis was about to say something but then thought better of it. He gave her a very suspicious look, one that let her know he knew she was full of shit. But apparently, he, like Jamie Griles, was used to talking to the police. He knew where to keep an eye out for traps and when to choose his words carefully.

"We're waiting for an answer," DeMarco said.

There was a brief moment wherein Sammy Curtis seemed to come to a decision. He sneered at them and then replaced it with a malicious smile. "I use it to keep the hair out of a girl's face when she's going down on me. Want me to show you?"

Kate had been expecting pushback, but nothing like that. She felt heat flush through her cheeks as DeMarco took one huge step toward him. She wasn't sure she had ever seen such fury in her partner's eyes.

"One chance," DeMarco said. "I'll give you one chance to take that back or I *will* place you under arrest."

Still, he gave that same sinister smile. And then, as if daring her to do something, he extended his arms, wrists up, with his hands clasped together. "Go ahead."

DeMarco looked back at Kate, giving her a very quick glance that said *what the hell is going on here?* Kate thought she knew, and it made her all the more certain that Curtis was familiar with the police and how things worked. But as she looked as his wrists, ready to be handcuffed, she wasn't sure if this pointed toward his guilt or innocence.

One way to find out, she thought.

"Sammy Curtis, we are hereby placing you under temporary arrest." She went through the remainder of the spiel as DeMarco placed her handcuffs on him and led him to their car.

When he was in the back seat, Kate and DeMarco met at the back of the car.

"He's playing chess," Kate said.

"How's that?"

"Me revealing that we knew about the ribbon in his truck was me making the first move, scooting a pawn up. You saw that he knew we shouldn't have been in his truck. But he let it go. It makes me think we might have found something else if he pushed in that direction."

"Then why willingly let us arrest him?"

"I don't know yet. Like I said . . . it's chess. And right now, we need to figure out what the next move is."

Chapter Nine

When they got to the station, Sheriff Gates didn't seem all that surprised that they had brought Sammy Curtis in. While Curtis was being checked in and shown to one of the station's two interrogation rooms, Gates pulled the files they had on him. There wasn't too much to report, but what was there told them all they needed to know.

Sammy Curtis had three counts of public misconduct. One of those came in the form of a fight outside of Esther's Place. The man he had been fighting was fifteen years older than him, the father of a fifteen-year-old girl Sammy had been texting with for a few weeks. Neither the girl in question nor Sammy ever admitted to a physical relationship, so the fight was the only thing he could be charged for. Besides that, Sammy had been the only one to sustain an injury—a slightly dislocated jaw.

When Kate handed the files back to Gates, the sheriff had a small frown on his face. "One thing you should know before you go too hard on him." He gathered his thoughts and sighed. "Please know that I am absolutely not making excuses for him. I am well aware that he is a wretched mess of a human being. And while he's been that way as far back as I can remember, it's gotten worse over the last three years or so. Did you notice all of the marks on his record have come in the past three years?"

"I did."

"He got busted cheating on his wife three years back. He was twenty-one at the time. The wife was a girl he dated in high school. They got married because she got pregnant. When they divorced, it got nasty. The wife got full custody of the daughter and they left town. I don't know where they went. But from what I hear, losing his daughter screwed him up. He's become almost intolerable to most people. He drinks way too much which I also hear is one of the other reasons the marriage ended."

"I appreciate the back story," DeMarco said. "But none of that is going to affect how we question him."

"Oh, no, I get it," Gates said. "Just thought you might want to know."

Kate and DeMarco headed back to the interrogation room with that little bit of history in mind. When they entered the room, Curtis was sitting in the chair behind the interrogation table as if he were simply hanging out with a friend. He looked calm and relaxed, as if this was old hat to him.

"It seems you know how this all works," DeMarco said. "You going to make us wait until you call your lawyer?"

"Nope. Don't have a lawyer."

"Want to tell us what you and Jamie Griles were up to last Wednesday night?"

"From what I gather, Jamie already told you."

"And you can confirm all of that?"

"Sure can. I can probably give you names of a few people at the party we went to if you need more proof. Got my bar tab from Esther's Place that night, too."

Kate chuckled. "And why couldn't you just tell us all of this when we were at your house?"

"Because I'm pissed off that people like me and Jamie always get placed under scrutiny for anything around here."

"Jamie Griles basically told us he has a thing for younger girls," DeMarco said. "And we've just been told about an inappropriate text thread you had with a minor not too long ago. So yes . . . you may get the stink eye from law enforcement when two young women are killed."

"So," Kate said, before she could give Curtis a chance to give a smart-assed exchange. "Let's say everything checks out and we can clear both you guys on Wednesday night. Can you tell me what you did Saturday?"

"Crashed at Jamie's place with this girl I've been seeing."

She of age?" Kate asked, already seeing the stories from both men lining up.

"Old enough. Legal, if that's what you're getting at."

DeMarco remained silent for a while. Kate could basically hear the cogs turning in her partner's head. She got DeMarco's attention and nodded to the table with an inquisitive rise of her eyebrows. DeMarco nodded, giving her full permission to go ahead with the questions.

"You know the names of both of the recent victims?"

"I knew Mariah was one. But I didn't know the other one was Kayla Peterson until Jamie told me on the phone."

"And when was that?"

"About twenty minutes before you two showed up, when he called me to let me know you were probably coming to my house."

"Did you know either of them personally?"

"No, not well."

"Mr. Curtis, I want you to think very hard about this. Do you have any idea why we might be interested in what you have to say?"

"Something about a pink cord you saw in my truck. And honestly, that's another reason I was pissed off. Even if you *did* have a warrant—and I know you didn't—that was none of your business."

"Well," DeMarco said, "there are certain details about this case that make the presence of that silk ribbon or cord or whatever it is very suspicious. I can't tell you the details, but—"

"It's this silk strand of string, feels like plastic almost," he said, interrupting her. He would not look at them when he spoke. He seemed to be looking far away, maybe trying to stare through the walls of the room. "It came in the mail a few weeks ago. A bracelet my daughter made. If you know about my record, I guess you know about my daughter and ex-wife. The bracelet broke. I had it hanging from my rearview mirror and accidentally snagged it. Little beads went everywhere. Had you looked hard enough, you would have probably seen some of them under the seat, too. So I took the little cord down and put it behind the seat, hoping to get around to fixing it."

Kate had to look away from him. She felt about an inch tall. She instantly regretted looking in the truck. It had been unethical and unnecessary. With a proper warrant, they could have looked it over inch by inch. But she'd had a feeling, a gut reaction to seeing the truck. And it looked as if it had ultimately been wrong... and now had her feeling guilty as hell.

"Again," DeMarco said. "Why not just tell us this at your house?"

"Because I'm an asshole. I wanted to waste your time."

DeMarco balled up her fist but turned around before she could say anything else or do anything rash.

"Mr. Curtis," Kate said, doing her best to keep her voice level. "There are two dead women, and a killer that is still out there. Is your little prank to get us to waste our time really worth that much to you? We could spend this time looking elsewhere."

"Like illegally going through people's vehicles?"

Kate had nothing else to say to this. She shook her head, gave DeMarco an apologetic glance, and then left the room.

She stood out in the hallway for about three minutes before DeMarco came out to join her. She looked irritated, but not angry. She leaned against the wall and looked at Kate for a moment, concerned. It was another of those moments where Kate could feel the torch being passed down.

"What's going on, Kate?" No *Agent Wise*, just *Kate.*

"Nothing. I made a stupid call and am currently regretting it. It isn't the first time."

"That's sort of what I'm getting at. You don't make stupid calls. In the time I've been working with you, I think you may have made two calls I maybe thought were unorthodox, but nothing like this. Looking in that truck without a warrant... that wasn't like you."

"I know. And I apologize."

"No, I mean it's okay. It turned out fine and honestly, it's not even that big of a deal. I'm just checking in. I know things have been hectic for you these past few months."

"I appreciate that. But I'm fine... really. Just a lapse in judgment."

DeMarco studied her for a moment before nodding, apparently satisfied with the explanation. Before turning back to the interrogation room, though, she turned back and frowned.

"I want to say something, and there's no way for it to *not* come off as confrontational. Just please know I don't mean it like it's going to sound."

"You don't have to explain. Go ahead."

"I knocked out two cases while you were out on maternity leave... one of which got the attention of quite a few people, including Director Duran. If I'm being honest, the main reason your snooping through Curtis's truck bothered me was because I was being selfish. I was worried about how it might look on me if it somehow got back to Duran or somehow messed up this case."

"So you need me to walk the straight and narrow on this one," Kate said. "That's what you mean."

"Yes." She looked almost guilty as she said it, unable to hold eye contact with Kate.

"DeMarco, it's perfectly fine. You have your future to plan out and look to. Meanwhile, I'm on the last lap of this thing. I get it."

"I just hate it . . . you know? I wouldn't be where I am right now if it weren't for you, but if I'm being honest . . ."

"Just say it. It's okay."

"I feel second-rate right now. I love having you on this case with me, but I feel like I'm playing dress-up or something."

"You *know* that's not the case. All that ass you kicked these last few months, you did that without me. You're in charge here, DeMarco. I'm just along for the ride."

"Thanks."

And with that, she turned away. Kate could tell she felt unsettled, but she let it go. They both had things they needed to work through. And if the past several months proved anything, it was that DeMarco was fully capable of handling such things on her own.

But one thing Kate had said made her feel as if it was *her* that was playing dress-up. *I'm just along for the ride.*

And if that were the case, just what in the hell was she doing here?

Chapter Ten

They called it a day and checked into one of the area's two hotels, a Sleep Inn that sat about five miles outside of Harper Hills. The ride from the station to the motel was mostly quiet. There was no real tension between them but things had been altered. It had been the sort of conversation that would forever change things between them. They both seemed to take it in stride though. The brief *goodnight* they shared with one another as they headed to their own individual rooms was polite enough, if not a bit strained.

Kate sat on the edge of her bed for a moment, simply thinking. She looked to her laptop bag and the folder sticking out of the front pocket. She knew she could go through the files, trying to find something that might link Kayla and Mariah, or Kayla to Sammy Curtis. If he could be linked to *both* victims, they might have something.

As it was, he was still at the station. Sheriff Gates had set two officers to look into verifying his stories about his whereabouts for the nights of both murders. He had all but been cleared of the murder of Mariah Ogden, but being that Griles was the only one who could really verify his whereabouts Saturday night, more effort was being put into it.

Her mind itched for the files. It would do her some good to dig into a case, on her own, just her, the papers and the forms. But her thoughts were all over the place—namely in feeling lost and out of place on this case. Hour by hour, she was starting to feel a little more useless, like this was indeed DeMarco's case and she was simply there for support.

When I found out I was somehow miraculously pregnant with Michael, I should have stopped.

It was a thought that had occurred to her since the first day of sitting in the hospital bed following his delivery. It was insane that she had given birth to a mostly healthy baby. If she'd needed a reminder, all she had to do was count the number of reporters who had asked for interviews. She should have taken the pregnancy as a sign—what sort of sign, she still wasn't sure. But certainly a sign that told her life as she knew it had come to an end and it was now time to slow down and start a different chapter.

Thinking of her pregnancy made her naturally think of Michael and Allen, back at home. She checked the time, saw that it was barely after ten, and decided it would be okay to call. She opted not to use FaceTime, as Allen couldn't stand it. He complained that it was too sci-fi for him, too invasive.

She called and Allen answered after the second ring. "Hey there, Miracle Mom."

She rolled her eyes. He'd been calling her that ever since the first headline had come out labeling her as such. He did it because it was endearing but also, he admitted, because he knew just how much it irked her.

"What are you boys up to tonight?" she asked.

"Michael partied a little too hard and went to bed at seven. Me . . . I'm living it up and catching up on my Netflix bingeing. Finally going to see what the big deal is about *Mr. Robot.* How about you? How's the case going?"

"Feels like nowhere, but it has the feel of one of those cases that is going to wrap itself up out of nowhere."

"How are you doing? Feel good to be back out there?"

She almost answered with a *yes*, but that would have been slightly dishonest. Instead, she hesitated a moment before saying: "I'm not sure yet. There are mixed emotions."

"You miss me that much, huh?"

"That's part of it," she said, ignoring his attempt at humor. "I do miss you. And I miss Michael, too. I'm here in the thick of it and I'm starting to understand that this is DeMarco's show now."

"She pushing you away?"

"God no. Nothing like that. I feel like a third wheel . . . even though there are only two of us. So that's a bad analogy. I feel *unnecessary.* And I'm starting to wonder if I made a mistake."

Allen was quiet, perhaps thinking over what he should say next. He was encouraging to a fault but he was also honest. He never really danced around what he was thinking; he usually just put it all out there. And when he waited this long to speak, it was usually because he was choosing his words carefully.

"Mistake or not... we both know you had to do it. You had to go back out there, to make sure you could still do it. I love you dearly, Kate... but we both know you never have any idea when to stop."

"I know. This is just... almost too much. I don't know how to explain it."

"Well, you're where again? North Carolina?"

"Yes."

"Then just come home. Call your director and let him know how you're feeling. No sense in going through this sort of turmoil if you aren't ready for it."

"I can't do that. I'm already here and gotten into it."

"But you just said you feel unnecessary."

"I know, but... I just—"

"Jesus, Kate. Is it that hard to let it go? I know you were incredibly good at that job, but you can't let it define you. Your life is different now. *Vastly* different. You've got a new son now. And yes, I still can't believe it, even when the words are coming out of my mouth. But we have a son together and, if I have my future play out the way I want, a *life* together. I've essentially retired and my job is slowly fading away. I don't understand why you can't do the same."

He was right about all if it, and she guessed that was why it hurt so much to hear it. "Allen, I can't just let it go. I'm getting signs and inclinations along the way that I need to, but it's all I ever knew."

"I'm aware of that," he said. His tone was firm yet caring. "But I want you to think of what that cost you. Ask Melissa what your obsession over your job did to her."

The comment bit deep and she nearly bit right back with a snarky comment. But she let it go because, of course, he was right.

After a tense five seconds passed, she gulped down the final impulse to argue and asked, "How's our little man?"

"He's good. He keeps looking around. You can tell he's looking for you, like he knows something is different around here. It's kinda cute."

"Kiss him for me, would you?"

"I'll do that. Get some sleep, Kate. Focus on the job, but we really need to figure this out."

"I know. I love you."

"Love you, too."

She killed the call and tossed the phone on the bed. She thought of Michael, of what he must be experiencing as he looked around the house, in search of his mother. She missed him, but in a way that made no real sense.

She thought of him as she brushed her teeth and readied herself for bed. She missed him in that she was not going to know what to do with herself when she woke up in the morning and would not be able to go check on him right away. She was going to miss that bright-eyed way he looked at her when she brought his morning bottle over to him.

And it was that string of thought that helped Kate to realize why she felt so at odds with missing him. Yes, she missed him. She missed her son, obviously. But she did not miss the daily grind of motherhood. She knew many women who claimed that maternity leave had been the best moments of their lives—just one-on-one time with their babies, a time to connect.

But Kate had never cared for it. She hadn't enjoyed it almost three decades ago with Melissa and she didn't care much for it now. While she loved the quality time, she did not like all of the sitting and making bottles, and the constant snuggling, playing, and speaking in a high-pitched voice.

Just thinking about it made her feel stifled and out of place.

My God, do I not fit in anywhere *now?*

It was a thought that latched on to her every thought as she lay down and tried to find sleep. As slumber eventually came, it was a question that evolved into yet another one—this one simpler and a bit more abrupt.

Am I a terrible mother?

That thought rested heavy on her, keeping sleep away a bit longer.

Chapter Eleven

He had driven by countless bars ever since he'd been old enough to drive. He had to admit the neon signs and the alluring ads with the half-naked women were indeed inviting, but they had also managed to push him away. No matter how hot the model in the ad was or how colorful those bright lights were, the thought of drinking beer always reminded him of his father. And when he was reminded of his father, his guts started to churn and a slight pain radiated out from behind his eyes until it enveloped his entire brain.

He was thinking of his father now, actually. He sat on his front porch, listening to the sounds of the night. They were close enough to bigger cities where the sounds of crickets weren't very loud. But they were present enough to remind him of where he had grown up. It had been about two hours south, in an even smaller town—all back roads and open fields. Growing up, the nights had been filled with a choir of crickets, tree frogs, and some weird-sounding bird his father had called a whippoorwill.

But there had been other sounds, too. Sounds that he still heard to this day, six years after his father had died. Those were the sounds of empty bottles rolling along the boards of their front porch, and the hissing crack of a can being opened.

He had never had a beer in his entire life. But when he saw commercials or movies where people were drinking and the noise of a top being pried from a bottle or the mouth of a can being punctured by the pull tab, he'd feel a chill.

On a few occasions, his father had forced him to steal beer from the little country store down the road from their house. It had usually been on Thursdays. By then, his father had blown through that week's paycheck. His father would send him with one dollar to pick up a loaf of bread, but to also swipe some of the cheap malt liquor that sat right beside the Pepsi drink box. Of course, poor old Mrs. Holt, the cashier and owner of the store, had never suspected a thing. So he would leave the store and bike the three-quarters of a mile back home with a loaf of bread and two pints of Night Train shoved into the waist of his pants.

And if he'd taken too long or had failed to get the booze, there would be beatings. It was usually just with his father's fists but every now and then, there was the belt. After a while, he'd stopped using the belt because a few teachers at school had notified the police when he had gone to school with welts on his arms.

Honestly, though, he barely remembered the beatings. He remembered the pain, sure, but it was the horror of not knowing what his father was capable of that had been the worst. It had been like living under a storm cloud, waiting for the lightning bolt to come down and fry you.

He'd hated his father for it then, but now that he was older and his father was dead and in the ground, that hatred usually morphed into a much bigger rage. And he never knew what to do with it. As of late, he'd found an outlet but wasn't quite sure if he would be able to keep at it.

Sadly enough, it was gullible old Mrs. Holt he was thinking of when he decided he needed to go out again—to release some of that rage again.

He knew where he would go. He'd known ever since he'd followed Kayla Peterson home. He checked his phone and saw that it was 11:45. He thought about maybe just waiting it out because it might be too late. But he knew this one pretty well, and knew if he acted quickly, there might still be time.

He took a deep breath of the chilled night air as he locked his front door and headed to his car, parked on the street. He drove out across Main Street and then took a left onto Miller Brook Road. Like most of the other little avenues in Harper Hills, the road was mostly bordered by trees. It made what he was about to do almost comically easy.

He found a little turnaround spot about four miles down Miller Brook Road. He pulled his car as far as he could into the spot without brushing up against any trees. Spots like these were abundant in Harper Hills thanks to the many hunters who wore down such spots during hunting season, as well as for the old dirt roads that had overgrown over time, but left behind their well-worn mouths all along the sides of the back roads.

He got out of the car and walked to the road. With no traffic coming (of course not, as it was now 12:02 a.m.), he walked to the middle of the road and saw that his car was well out of sight. Someone would really have to be looking for it in order to see it. Satisfied with this, he walked back to the edge of the road and then into the woods. He stayed relatively close to the road, wanting to know if anyone came by.

Maybe he *was* too late. She usually didn't stay out too late, especially on weeknights.

Thinking of her, he reached into his pocket and fingered the old plastic cord.

He came to the driveway about three minutes later. Somewhere in the distance, he could hear a dog barking. But there was no threat nearby. He was going to be able to do this quickly and quietly. He would—

As he started trailing along the edge of the shallow driveway, a car turned into it. He stopped and dropped to the ground, watching the lights pass by. Through a tangle of weeds and roughage, he could see her car, barely illuminated by its own headlights.

It was her. He had timed it perfectly after all. Well, maybe not perfectly. He was going to have to haul ass if he wanted to catch her. From the way it looked, this one was going to work itself out just like the night he'd killed Kayla Peterson.

He waited until he saw the red cherry glow of her brake lights. The night went quiet as the engine of the car was turned off. Leaping out into the weeds along the edge of the driveway was exhilarating; he imagined it was what a lion or tiger must feel like when it is on the brink of a hunt.

He moved quickly, reaching into his pocket for that cord. The old familiar texture of it sent a million different thoughts through his head, most of which were killed off the moment he saw her shape walking through the night, toward the house. Yes, this was going to be almost exactly like Kayla Peterson. The thought of it brought a smile to his face. His heart felt like it might beat right out of his chest.

He moved quickly, his sneakers not making much of a noise as he passed by her car. He could hear the crunch of gravel under his feet, but it was slight. There was no way she would hear it, as she was already standing at the front door, reaching into her purse for her keys.

He reached the porch, and it was there that his urgency gave him away. One of the porch steps creaked under his weight. She seemed to hear this because she slowly turned around. In the dark, he could see the concern and slight alarm on her face. Her turning and hearing him ended up making his job much easier.

At the last moment, he lunged. The cord was outstretched tight in his hands and it slipped around her neck from the front quite easily. He drew it tight across her neck as he heard the deep inhale of what would be a scream if it came back out. But he fell on top of her, twisting her around. When they fell to the porch floor, he again got lucky in that her purse softened the blow. It was barely a noise at all, likely impossible to hear from inside unless someone was standing right there at the door.

He lay on top of her and found that it was almost comfortable. His weight pinned her to the porch. She wriggled beneath him, but he outweighed her by fifty pounds or more. Probably closer to seventy-five. She was tiny, though there was a lot of fight in her. He wrapped the cord even tighter around his right hand and pulled harder.

She grunted and huffed, but nothing more. Then, less than a minute later, she stopped moving altogether.

He stayed there on top of her for another thirty seconds or so, pulling tightly at the cord, just to be sure. When he was certain she was dead, he rolled off of her and got to his feet. He looked down at her for about three seconds before he leaped down the porch steps and retreated back toward the forest.

He found his car where he'd left it exactly eight minutes ago. He got inside, cranked it to life, and pulled back out into the road completely unseen.

Chapter Twelve

Kate wasn't surprised that she had not slept well. She couldn't recall a time she had been so at odds with herself since her husband had died nearly nine years ago. After that, there had, of course, been multiple questions about what her life would look like after he was gone. Ultimately, she had chosen to go even harder at work. She had regretted it for about a week, but had ended up burying that regret.

It was that regret she found herself thinking of as she got dressed for the day, unable to go back to sleep at 5:40. She had found herself at another crossroads, and she had pointed herself toward her career. But this time, she had not gone too far down that path. This time, there was still a chance to turn around and do the right thing.

She meant what she had told Allen last night, though. She had started this case, so she would finish it. She had never quit on a case, not even when she had been struck down with the flu during a triple homicide case back in 2003. She'd finish this case out and then she could revisit the decision.

If anything, it actually gave her more motivation to wrap the case up. As she leafed through the case files on the edge of the bed, she kept coming back to the trio of girls they had spoken to about Kayla Peterson. She'd had some sort of feeling about Olivia Macintyre when they'd been sitting there in Esther's Place. She didn't think the girl had been completely dishonest, but she *had* seemed uncomfortable. It wasn't a stretch to think she might have been hiding something.

She was about to type a note into her phone to make sure speaking to Olivia was one of the first things they did today, but she was interrupted by a knock at her door. She answered and found DeMarco standing on the other side. She was dressed, had a coffee in her hand, and dead-set look on her face.

She skipped good morning formalities and even before she spoke a word, Kate knew what she was going to say. She'd seen that look before, not only on DeMarco, but on other agents as well.

The next words out of DeMarco's mouth proved Kate right.

"There's been another murder."

⚜ ⚜ ⚜

The body was that of Vanessa Fenton, a nineteen-year-old local. Her body had been discovered by her father as he had left for work that morning. The residence was yet another one that was tucked out in the woods. It was less than five miles away from the hotel Kate and DeMarco were staying in.

This was the only information they knew for sure as they made their way up onto the porch of the Fenton residence.

As Kate and DeMarco fell in beside Sheriff Gates, the sounds of the girl's parents could be heard inside. The father seemed absolutely devastated, his complaints coming in screams and moans. The mother's sorrow was more grounded, a low and almost rhythmic sort of droning cry.

Gates didn't have to say a single word. The three of them looked down to the body and saw pretty much the same thing they'd seen with Kayla Peterson. Her eyes were open, wide and terrified. There was fresh bruising all around her neck. The attack was so recent that there seemed to be an indentation within some of the bruising, evidence that some sort of cord or rope had been used to strangle her.

The only real difference was that Vanessa Fenton had struggled a bit. It was evident in the scratch marks and slight tears along her cheeks. Her face had been rubbed hard against the porch at some point during her murder. There were little streaks of blood on the wood, partially dried, to prove this.

"I wonder if the scratch marks indicate some sort of physical abuse outside of the murder," Gates said.

"If you're talking about sexual assault, I doubt it," DeMarco said. "Her pants are still on. For a guy to rape her and then put her pants back on . . . that's a lot of effort."

"And a lot of time. This guy is apparently working very quickly. Two girls, right at their front doors. He's timing it out perfectly. Even if he had rape in mind, I don't think he'd have had the time."

"The medical examiner can rule that out for us pretty swiftly," DeMarco added.

Kate looked back down into the yard, to the driveway that led back out to the road. She could just barely see it in the morning light—which, she assumed, meant it was pretty much invisible at night.

"I think he's been on foot every time," Kate said, thinking out loud.

"How's that?" Gates asked.

"Even if he was driving with his headlights off, what are the chances that she wouldn't have noticed a car coming in behind her?"

"It's a good point," DeMarco said. "He was either on foot or came in behind Vanessa in his own car and she *knew* it."

"As in, he was invited?" Gates asked.

"Yes. But honestly, I think Agent Wise is right on this one. I think he was on foot. Maybe came into the yard through the forest to either side of the house. It could have worked well with Kayla Peterson, too."

"If he *is* on foot, it makes his timing even stronger," Kate said. "Calculating the time it might take to walk through the forest at night..."

DeMarco cocked her head, thinking. "But maybe it wasn't that far of a walk. Maybe he parked his car somewhere nearby and then walked just a tiny bit through the woods. Maybe he walked to the edge of the yard, ducked down in the trees, and just waited for her to get home."

Gates was nodding, clearly growing to accept the idea. "And for someone like that, it would have to be someone who knows the town well. He'd have to know the roads that would be dead at certain hours, maybe even some of the pullover spots the hunters use during deer season."

"She's nineteen, right?" Kate said. "High school or college?"

"College," Gates said. "A freshman at Duke."

"Hold on," DeMarco said. "Kayla was home for a wedding, which makes sense. But why would Vanessa be home? Duke has got to be at least an hour and a half away, right?"

"Right," Gates said. "But you forget, it's November. It's fall break, or Thanksgiving break, or whatever you want to call it. The wedding Kayla was in town for is this weekend. Just a happy coincidence."

Seems like an unhappy one to me, Kate thought.

As Kate and DeMarco continued to study the scene, the front door to the house opened up. Officer Smith stepped out, closed the door, and let out a deep breath. It was evident that he had been doing his best to hold in tears while speaking with the parents.

"We need to move her body," Smith said. "Where the hell is the coroner?"

"About five minutes out, if I had to guess," Gates said.

"Who's with the family right now?" DeMarco asked.

"There are two other officers inside with them," Gates said. "One of them is the oldest lady on our force and just happens to have a background in grief counseling."

"Still," Smith said. "Please... leave them be for now. In the meantime, I think I may have gotten some information from them that can help with your investigation. According to the mother, Vanessa was out with a friend last night—most of yesterday, actually. They drove up to Duke so Vanessa could show her friend around, came back and had dinner right here, with her folks. They then went out to see a movie over in Glensville. Mrs. Fenton showed me the text Vanessa sent her at nine fifty-two to let her know the movie had let out, and that she had her friend were going to get some pie at Esther's Place, and then she'd be home around midnight or so."

"Is that common?" Kate asked. "Dessert at the same place shit-kickers like Jamie Griles and Sammy Curtis go to drink?"

"Yeah, it is," Gates said. "I've grumbled to management about it to no end. But they do a good job over there of keeping things lawful and tidy. Bar on one side, diner on the other. The diner is usually pretty dead after nine or so, but a few late-night partiers will go in from time to time with the munchies."

"Do we have a name for the friend she spent all day with?"

"Jenna Marshall," Smith said. "Give me a second and I can get the address."

Smith left the porch in a hurry, as if he were glad to have an excuse to be away from the body. Kate mulled over everything Smith had just told them as he marched out to the car and punched something into the dashboard console unit.

"Three girls, three different colleges," Kate said.

"Strange, right?" DeMarco said. "A town like this, where a lot of the kids don't even bother with college, you can't help but wonder if they're being targeted *for* that."

"All due respect," Gates said, "I think that's a dangerous and, if I'm being honest, *snotty* way to look at it."

"Of course it is," Kate said. "But right now, it's a strong possible motivator, based on the similarities in the victims."

"Speaking of similarities," DeMarco said, "the three young ladies we spoke to that knew Kayla Peterson were a varied bunch. What can you tell us about Jenna Marshall before we go tell her that her friend was killed?"

"As far as I know, she's a clean kid. Her parents are considered very well-to-do. Her dad works from home for some big software company, I think. The Marshalls live in one of the handful of upscale neighborhoods in town."

As he wrapped up this explanation, a slight dinging noise sounded out on the porch. Kate and DeMarco instinctively reached for their phones but realized at the same time that it was not a sound either of their phones made.

"Not mine, either," Gates said.

With that, all three of them looked down to Vanessa Fenton. Her purse, still partially trapped beneath her, seemed to give off the softest of glows. Curiously, DeMarco reached down and shifted the purse. Using just the tips of her fingers as to not leave prints everywhere, she removed the girl's cell phone.

"She just got a text," DeMarco said, showing them the phone.

On the screen, Kate saw a text that had just come through. The contact was listed simply as JENNA. The message read: *Hey crazy bitch. Just checking in. Crazy night huh? You ok?*

"That sounds . . . troublesome," DeMarco said.

"Agreed," Kate said. "Let's so see where Smith is with getting us that address."

She looked back down to the bruising on Vanessa Fenton's neck one last time before walking down toward the patrol car to start what she was already feeling would be a very long day.

CHAPTER THIRTEEN

It wasn't even 8:30 in the morning, and Kate found herself listening to yet another person weep and wail in extreme sorrow. It was definitely not the way to start a day and she decided that if she did decide to hang up her career after this case, it would be one of the few things she would *not* miss about the job.

She and DeMarco were sitting in the Marshalls' living room. They had broken the news to Jenna Marshall and her parents ten minutes ago. Jenna's response had been an immediate break where she had screamed and wept hard enough to nearly hyperventilate. She had asked to be excused, followed by her parents.

Now, as Jenna's sobs started to soften from elsewhere in the house, her father came back into the living room. He sat down in a large recliner and looked to both of them with disbelief.

"Sorry," he said. "She's obviously having a rough time with this."

"Of course," DeMarco said. "As I'm sure you can understand, Vanessa's parents are absolutely broken-hearted right now and it would not be in anyone's best interests to question them. We thought your daughter would be the next best bet."

"Sure. And she understands that. She wants to help, she just—"

"I'm fine."

They all turned and saw Jenna walking into the living room. She looked fragile, but there was fire in her eyes, too. Her grief had quickly taken a turn toward a need for vengeance, and it was more than evident in her eyes.

"Let me help. However I can help, I will. I want to know who killed her."

"That's exactly why we're here," DeMarco said. "Anything you can tell us about last night—anything out of the ordinary or alarming—would be helpful. That or anything at all you might know about people who held grudges against Vanessa."

"I can't think of anyone who would want her dead, if that's what you mean. Sure, there are some girls around town that might have a beef with her from petty high school stuff, but nothing serious."

"Did she have any boyfriends that you knew of?"

"Two different ones in high school. But one of them moved to Canada and the other one is honestly the sweetest guy you'd ever meet. He's playing football for Texas Tech."

"We understand she took you to her campus yesterday," DeMarco said. "Did she introduce you to anyone she knew at college?"

"We ran into a girl who lives on her hall, but that was it. She just showed me around campus, showed me a few places she hangs out, that sort of thing."

"What kind of mood was she in yesterday?" Kate asked.

"That's what's... so sad about it," Jenna said, fighting back tears. "She was in such a *great* mood yesterday. We were singing at the top of our lungs on the way back. She was excited about her mom's lasagna for dinner last night, and the movie we saw was really good. It was a pretty great day."

"And what about after the movie?" DeMarco said. "We saw a text from Vanessa to her mother saying you were going to Esther's for pie."

Jenna looked quickly to the floor, a surefire sign of guilt. Before Kate could even ask what had caused the reaction, Jenna's mother spoke up.

"Jenna... you did what?"

"Mom, it's not a big deal..."

"I'm sorry," DeMarco said. "Can someone please fill me in here? Is *pie at Esther's* code for something else?"

"No," Mr. Marshall said. "Last year, during the summer, Jenna was caught purchasing marijuana from someone in the women's restroom at Esther's. Since then we've asked her to stay away from the crowd that was dealing, as well as from Esther's in general."

"We really did just have pie," Jenna said.

"If I may be so bold, the text you sent to Vanessa this morning suggested otherwise. Unless the pie you had was incredibly good."

"What text?" Mrs. Marshall said.

Jenna took a moment to get words out. The look on her face was a mixture of embarrassment, sadness, and any other number of shameful emotions. "I'm sorry," she said. "But you know what? There's nothing to do around here and I had to sit and watch while my best friend went to college! She came back and yeah ... we wanted to party and celebrate."

"What did you do, Jenna?" her father asked.

"With all due respect," DeMarco said, "we need any information she has right now if we want to find who did this. If there are punishments or longer discussions to be had on the matter, I'd appreciate it if they wait until we're gone." She then returned her attention to Jenna and gave the girl a pleading look. "Anything at all you can tell us would be very helpful."

Jenna sighed and, through tears, confessed. "It was just a few mushrooms," she said. "Nothing too serious. We got 'em, went and parked out in Meyers Field, and took them."

Mrs. Marshall made a little noise of shock. Mr. Marshall got to his feet and stormed off into the adjoining kitchen. Jenna watched them go and wiped a stray tear away from her cheeks.

"Guys, I'm so sorry ..."

"Jenna, did you know the person you brought them from?" Kate asked.

"Yeah. I don't want to give her name, I don't want to snitch."

"I understand that. Tell me this, though: is it someone you trust? Someone you're familiar with?"

"I don't know her well enough to say I'd *trust* her, but I know her. And if you're asking if I think she'd be the type to kill someone, I'd say no. She's one of those ditzy blonde plastic types. The idea of her even *thinking* of killing someone—or of even throwing a punch—is laughable."

Kate and DeMarco shared a look, a sort of telepathic message to one another through their expressions. It said: *Probably not worth looking into, but let's put a pin in it.*

"Did you run into anyone last night that seemed to have an attitude?" DeMarco asked. "Anyone who seemed to be angry at you?"

"No. There was this one guy that hit on us after the movie, right there in front of the concessions in the lobby. We rejected him, obviously. He seemed a little hurt by it, but he went right back to his group of friends. We never even thought twice about it."

"And how did the night end, exactly?" Kate asked.

"Well, we took her car to the movie after dinner at her house, and she drove to the movies, then to Esther's. She dropped me off right around midnight ... maybe a little later. And that was it. That was the last time I saw her."

A thought occurred to Kate, one they had mentioned almost in passing once before. But now that there were three victims so close in age, it seemed very important.

"Vanessa was nineteen, right?"

Jenna nodded. "Turned nineteen about a month ago, actually."

"So she graduated high school when? Last year?"

"Yeah, we both graduated last year."

"Jenna... do you know the names Mariah Ogden or Kayla Peterson?"

"I know both of them. Not all that well. But I do know about what happened to Mariah. It was awful, huh?" Her eyes bounced back and forth between the agents and started to widen. "Wait... was Kayla killed, too?"

"She was," DeMarco said. "And the fact that you didn't know yet tells me the gossip circles haven't covered the entire town yet. So let's keep that quiet for now, okay?"

Jenna nodded, furrowing her brow like someone who was trying to figure out an incredibly hard problem. She was trying to digest it all, trying to understand.

"Mariah was nineteen, too," Kate said. "Was she in your graduating class? Same high school?"

"Yeah, there's only one high school around here. Everyone in Harper Hills and anywhere about twenty miles or so away goes to it."

"And what about Kayla?"

"No. She was a grade above me. She graduated the year before Vanessa and I."

"Do you recall Vanessa ever having any sort of connections with either Kayla or Mariah?"

"She had some classes with Mariah. But they were never really friends. Cordial and polite, you know? As for Kayla, I don't know that Vanessa ever spoke a word to her. Different grade, different circles, you know?"

It shut a lot of doors as far as theories went, but it also planted the seeds for a few more. Kate digested it all and sat back in her chair, giving DeMarco the indication that she was done and it was all hers again. After some thought and thick tension brewing in the air between Jenna and her parents, DeMarco decided to get up. When she headed for the front door, she handed Mrs. Marshall one of her business cards.

"If she thinks of anything else, please allow her to call. She's been a big help."

Mrs. Marshall gave a distant-sounding *"of course"* but it was clear that her mind was elsewhere . . . likely on feeling duped by her daughter in terms of where she had spent the last part of the previous night.

Mr. Marshall escorted them to the door, but he said nothing either. He gave them a lifeless nod as they made their exit and then closed the door behind them.

"Man, I'd hate to be Jenna right now," DeMarco said.

"All things considered, I'd rather be her than Vanessa Fenton."

"Good point." She remained quiet until they reached their car, and then asked, "I'm wondering who we can talk to at the school. Maybe someone who can dig up some sort of link between the three victims. Maybe the superintendent."

"It's a great idea," Kate said. "But if you don't mind a helpful tip . . ."

DeMarco grinned. "It might be my case, but I'm still willing to learn."

Kate could essentially feel the resentment coming off of the comment. Maybe things weren't as smoothed over between the two of them as she thought. Still, she decided to go ahead and offer her advice.

"With a small town like this one, your best bet is to go with the principal. The superintendent is going to want to cover his ass and the school board's ass. Even if he *does* know something, he'd be hesitant to tell us because it might point to something they missed. Looks bad on a lot of people. The principal, however, usually tends to be more worried about the students and the well-being of the school."

DeMarco chuckled as she got behind the wheel of the car. "Small-town politics. Man, you'd think it would be easier in a small town like this."

"As we can see with the three dead girls within the last week, small-town life isn't always as it seems."

That said, DeMarco pulled away from the curb in front of the Marshalls' house while Kate called up Gates to get the phone number of the high school principal.

Chapter Fourteen

The principal of Stateside High School, located almost directly between Harper Hills and Glensville, was a fifty-year-old woman named Deborah Robinson. She had happily agreed to meet with Kate and DeMarco but insisted it not be at the school. Instead, she suggested a small coffee shop five miles away from the school—a twenty-minute drive outside of Harper Hills.

When she came into the coffee shop, she walked quickly over to where Kate and DeMarco sat. Deborah Robinson was a slender African American woman who could have passed for thirty-five on a good day. When she sat down across from them, she looked worried but unfazed. She extended her hand to both of them as a quick round of formal introductions were made.

"I appreciate you meeting me here," she said. "Tomorrow is the last day of public school before the Thanksgiving break and word is getting around about what happened to Kayla Peterson. They already know about Mariah Ogden, of course. You can feel the uneasiness in the halls. It's a very strange vibe."

"I'm sorry to tell you, it's going to get worse," DeMarco said. "Earlier this morning, the body of Vanessa Fenton was found on her parents' front porch. She was killed in the same way as Kayla and Mariah."

Even before she was halfway through the news, Deborah's face seemed to fold inward a bit. She covered her mouth and shook her head slowly. "This just can't be," she said softly.

"This makes three victims in under a week," Kate said. "We've just spoken with one of Vanessa Fenton's friends, a girl named Jenna Marshall. She said as far as she can remember, there's no real link between any of these three girls. I was hoping to speak to you to see if you, as a school official, might know something she didn't."

Deborah thought about it for a moment and again slowly shook her head. "If there's a connection, it's not an obvious one. Now, for the sake of full honesty, I have to say I did not know Kayla Peterson all that well. And even if I did, I believe she graduated two years ago so I don't know that I would be able to recall much."

"But you remember Mariah and Vanessa?"

"Oh yes. Mariah, in particular. She used her free period during senior year to help out in the office. Filing mail, making copies, things like that."

"When you hear those three names, you get no alarms or ill thoughts of any kind?"

"No... no, I'm sorry. I just don't know if I can help you there."

"That's quite all right," DeMarco said. "So let's go another route. Can you think of anyone over the past two years who was something of a troublemaker? Not just someone who cuts up in class or gets caught dealing drugs or defacing property. I'm talking about someone that was sort of seen as a threat or a risk."

"There were one or two, yes. Just last year, we had to call the police to have two boys removed for fighting. One of the boys got knocked unconscious and was in a coma for about two days. But in terms of someone that I would have thought might be a killer later on... no. I never saw a student like that."

"Ms. Robinson, how long have you been the principal at Stateside High?" Kate asked.

"This will be my ninth year."

"If you look way back in your memory a few years, do you remember two boys named Jamie Griles and Sammy Curtis?"

Deborah gave a small roll of her eyes and nodded. "Oh yeah. Griles got suspended once for groping a girl in the hallway. He was bad news. I hate to say that about a kid that has gone through my school, but it's true."

"Do you recall if he ever showed violent tendencies?" Kate asked. Sure, they had pretty much ruled him out due to his alibis, but there was never any harm in double-checking these sorts of things.

"Not that I can remember. Jamie Griles wasn't the type you had to worry about getting into a fight. He was the type you needed to worry about being in a confined space with a female."

"What about Sammy Curtis?" DeMarco asked.

"I think the worst he ever got caught doing was smoking on school property. I don't recall him ever getting into much real trouble. But he did hang out with crowds I would have considered *bad*."

"I'm sure you can see the link we're trying to dig into here," DeMarco said. "Three girls, all having graduated from the same high school within one year of one another. The school itself sort of becomes the link."

"So we have to check students you considered high risk or even just troublemakers," Kate added. "Maybe even beyond students. If you can think of any staff members or faculty that might have had some issues in the last year or so, that might be worth looking into as well."

Deborah's eyes narrowed and she started to look uneasy. Her hand had ventured back up to her mouth, as if it wasn't sure how to respond. "Yes, but there's no hard proof. And I'm not one to gossip."

"I can understand that," Kate said. "But we can frame it as speaking to an ex-employee that may have had contact with one or more of the victims. It doesn't have to be a confrontational meeting. Not at first, anyway."

"Howard Schuler," Deborah said.

"Who is that?" DeMarco asked.

"He was a guidance counselor who was fired last year. There were rumors about how he was conducting himself outside of school. There was never any proof, but the rumors had gotten bad enough for parents to call the school to ask questions."

"What were the rumors?"

"That he was being a little too friendly with students. There had been rumors around here for years that he would sometimes stare at girls a little too long. Maybe placing a hand on their shoulder or knee when they came to his office. The hell of it was that he got away with it because he's a good-looking man. A lot of the girls had these innocent schoolgirl crushes on him. But then I and some of the other faculty started to hear about how he would show up at house parties thrown by the students on weekends. We had meetings with him to try to bring it to light, but he never confessed. None of the students we approached would, either."

"Then why was he fired?" Kate asked.

"We got two different calls within the space of a month that Howard had been seen at parties, taking beer inside. Of course, high schoolers can't buy beer, so we assume he was supplying the beer in exchange for their secrecy. He'd get them booze if no one ratted him out for being at the parties."

"But there was no solid proof?" Kate asked.

"No. But I suppose he had just heard enough of it. When we called him into a meeting about it, he sort of blew up. Said he was insulted and hurt. I thought he was going to quit right there and then but he did not. He stayed in school for another week or so, but all of the rumors had basically tanked his professional relationship with a lot of the teachers. After a while, it just became too distracting, so we had to let him go."

"Did you believe the rumors?" DeMarco asked.

"I didn't at first. But then there was this terrible car accident last summer. A junior was killed on his way home one night. The autopsy showed that he had a ridiculously high blood-alcohol level. The cops asked his girlfriend where he got the alcohol but she refused to tell anyone. Got the same reaction when she was asked where they had been coming from."

"You think it was Howard Schuler?" Kate asked.

"I wouldn't go so far as to state it from the front of a courtroom, but it seemed like it. When the cops later found out some of the kids the junior boy had been hanging out with, one of them was linked to Schuler in that his parents were one of the calls we'd gotten in the past about him."

"What else do you know about the crash?" DeMarco asked.

"Not enough to be accurate," Deborah said. "You'd be better off going to the police with that."

The agents nodded in unison and Kate could feel the interview coming to a close. "Ms. Robinson... can you think of *anyone* who might have had any sort of grudge against these three girls? Anything at all?"

"No," she said quickly. "Things like this don't happen here. You know, we're in North Carolina and pretend as much as we want, there's still racism around and I see it in the schools. And there are still sexually aggressive boys in my halls, and girls that sleep around just to get attention. But it's a pretty decent community. For every *one* troubled kid, I can point you to twenty great ones. This... this sort of thing just doesn't happen around here and, quite frankly, it's starting to get everyone scared. When news of Vanessa Fenton gets out, things could get very scary indeed."

Kate had guessed this, too. And it was currently sitting at the top of her large pile of reasons to wrap this case as soon as possible.

⚜ ⚜ ⚜

Gates set a thin case file down on the table in front of Kate and DeMarco. They were sitting in what served as a reserve office in the Harper Hills police department. It was a plain room with only the table and three chairs sitting around it. Gates sat down in the other chair, eyeing the file he had just given them.

"That's the file you were asking for," he said. DeMarco picked it up and opened it even though Gates started to roll through the specifics. "Jonathan Bowen, sixteen years old. Died in an automobile crash on July seventh last summer. It's believed he died almost on impact. I won't get into the grisly details, as you can read it for yourself."

"Deborah Robinson said there was a girlfriend," Kate said. "Was she also in the car?"

"She was. Her boyfriend died right away and she came out with nothing more than five stitches on her forehead and a concussion." He hesitated here and then asked: "Before you get to it yourself... did Robinson tell you about the other car?"

"No," Kate said, already starting to get a sinking feeling in her stomach.

"A mother and her two kids, one of whom had just turned two. All three died."

"Oh my God."

The room went quiet for a while, the silence broken only by the sound of DeMarco turning through the pages in the file. When she was done, she handed them over to Kate. Kate took the folder even though she did not want to see what was inside.

"Was no one ever busted for supplying Jonathan Bowen with the alcohol?" DeMarco asked.

"No. And we put one hell of an investigation into it. But in a town like this, if people decide they aren't going to talk... well, that's just about the end of it."

"Was Howard Schuler ever questioned?"

"He was one of the first. But you have to understand... it's almost impossible to prove something like that. I'm sure Robinson told you that there had been speculation that Schuler would show up at teen house parties, possibly hooking them up with alcohol. There are even some things that came in through the station that she may not have heard."

"Such as?"

"Schuler paying a seventeen-year-old girl for oral sex. Mind you, I said *speculation.* The call we got was from a teenager and though we looked into it, there was, of course, no proof."

"If you were to push all the rumors and speculation aside, what sort of man would you say Howard Schuler is?" Kate asked.

"Just like any other guy, I guess. Never makes much noise, plays by the rules. Some might say he loved his job but that's where the rumors come in. I think most men would love their jobs if they had young girls giving him glances every now and then."

"What's *your* opinion?" DeMarco asked. "Do you think he supplied Jonathan Bowen with alcohol?"

"He could have. But I just can't say for sure. You have to think of how that system would work. Think about being a teenager at a party where an adult as brought in a lot of beer. If someone you know leaves that party, gets in an accident that kills him and three others, are you going to step forward? Are you going to narc out the adult and, in the process, yourself for being at that party?"

It was an easy answer, but it did not make it any easier for Kate to accept. "He still live around here?" she asked.

"Just outside of town, yeah. Ironically, from what I understand, he's teaching on one of these online classroom deals. But why the interest in him? Even if he *was* buying kids beer, it certainly doesn't make him a killer."

"It doesn't," DeMarco said. "But we have an employee at a school who was surrounded by rumors of inappropriate behavior with young girls. And it's the same school these three victims all attended, a year or so before he was eventually let go. Even if he's not the killer, it's a hell of a good place to start."

Kate couldn't have said it better herself. She closed up the file on Jonathan Bowen and placed it back on the table. "Can you get us the address for Howard Schuler?"

"Sure," Gates said, getting up and taking the Bowen file with him. Before he left, he turned back to them and, after a deep sigh, added: "By the way, the medical examiner called just before you got here. Your hunch was right. No evidence of sexual assault on Vanessa Fenton. Just the scrapes on her face and whatever he's using to strangle them."

His face seemed to contort for a moment and he suddenly had to look away.

"You okay, Sheriff?" Kate asked.

"No. Actually, I'm pretty fucking far from it. I just hope..." Again, he paused and struggled with emotion.

"What is it?" Kate pressed.

"I just hope the two of you are the ones to find this guy. Because if I find him first, I'm afraid I might end up losing my job."

With that heavy comment, Gates left the room. Kate knew it was just her own stretched emotions, but she thought she could actually feel the tense and chilly sensation of the sheriff's rage settling down over the room.

Chapter Fifteen

It was 1:35 when DeMarco parked their car in Howard Schuler's driveway. It was a relatively nice house, sitting on the edge of a small picturesque neighborhood. Kate knocked on the door and when it opened, she was a bit surprised by the man who answered. She remembered Robinson saying that some of the high school girls had experienced little crushes on Schuler. She hated to think of people in such a way, but seeing Schuler for the first time made it rather hard for her to see a teenage girl finding him attractive.

Schuler looked to be nearing forty. He had a receding hairline that he tried to make look more natural by having his long hair pulled back in a messy surfer-type ponytail. His beard, though well-maintained, looked odd and out of place on his face. When he saw the two professional-looking women on his porch, he tried to seem aloof. He took an exaggerated step back and widened his eyes.

"Good afternoon, ladies," he said. "What can I do for you today?"

DeMarco once again took the lead, showing her badge and showing she was not at all impressed with his carefree attitude. "Agents DeMarco and Wise, FBI. We're investigating a string of recent murders in the area. Young women who were recent graduates of the high school you were fired from two years ago."

"Wow," Schuler said, any hope of playing the remainder of this meeting as a carefree guy now dashed. "You just go right for the jugular, huh?" He sighed and then stepped to the side, waving them through the doorway. "Come on in. I have, of course, heard the news. Two girls, right?"

"It's now three," Kate said.

"Jesus."

He closed the door behind them and Kate found that Schuler kept a clean little bachelor pad. The surfer ponytail made sense, as most everything in his home had a grungy sort of beach or island vibe to it, right down to the surf contest print on his living room wall. In looking around, she also spotted the two beer bottles on the coffee table, one of which was empty. The little water ring around the half-full one told her that it was a recent one.

"When you were a guidance counselor, did you know Kayla Peterson or Mariah Ogden?" DeMarco asked.

"I knew Kayla, yes. She wasn't sure if college was right for her or not, so we had several meetings to try to figure it out. That would have been her junior year, I believe."

"What about Vanessa Fenton?" Kate asked.

Schuler seemed to actually think quite hard about it and slowly started to nod his head. "The name does sound familiar, but I can't place a face."

"I take it she didn't attend any of the parties you slipped into?" DeMarco asked.

Any remaining traces of the cool-teacher vibe Schuler was trying to hold onto were demolished with that comment. "That's a low blow."

"Is it?" DeMarco asked. "Please forgive me, Mr. Schuler. We have three girls that have all been killed in the space of a week. Surely, as someone who has worked with teens, you understand that we don't have the luxury of time. Therefore, we have to be blunt about certain things."

Schuler nodded and plopped down in a plush recliner that took up about half of the living room's back wall. "Fine then," he said. "I'm happy to help find whoever is responsible for this. And if I have to be humiliated for poor choices I made—"

Kate wasn't interested in hearing him try to twist the situation to make himself the victim, so she interrupted him.

"Mr. Schuler, when you attended these parties, were there ever any students there that took exception to you being there?" she asked. "That is, did you perhaps make some kids upset or mad?"

"Not that I'm aware of." It was obvious that he was choosing his words carefully as he proceeded, clearly not wanting to set a trap for himself. "I think, as sad as it seems, some of the kids thought it was cool that someone from school was there."

"And why, exactly, did you go to these parties?"

He crossed his arms and, for a moment, looked like a pouting teenager. "I've apologized for these mistakes to the point of absurdity. I was in a bad place and was wanting to relive my youth. I used to tell people all the time that I loved being a guidance counselor rather than a teacher because there's more of an intimate connection—and no, I don't mean that in the perverted twisted way people like to think. The relationship between a student and a guidance counselor is more like a friendship than a teacher-student one, I think. To some of the kids, I was just another friend who had come to hang out."

"Were you ever inappropriate with the girls at these parties?" DeMarco asked.

Schuler waited a beat before he responded. He was getting angry and doing everything he could to keep his cool. "No, I was not. And as former educator, I am well aware that you have to ask that question and *why* you would ask that question. But no, that was never even on my radar when I went to those parties."

"Did you perhaps bring alcohol to these parties?" Kate asked, looking to the two bottles on his coffee table—a beer and a half gone before two in the afternoon.

"No."

"Are you sure?" DeMarco asked. "Maybe that was why the kids were always so happy to see you when you showed up at these parties."

"Wait... hold on. You came in here telling me you had questions about the murders that were going on."

"Oh, we're getting there," DeMarco said.

Schuler looked back and forth between them, his face growing madder and more alarmed by the moment. "You... you mean to tell me you think I'm a suspect?"

"I never once said such a thing," DeMarco said.

"Me neither," Kate added.

"So what do these mistakes have to do with—"

"Tell us what really happened with the accident that killed Jonathan Bowen, a mother, and her two kids," DeMarco said.

The cool and collected version of Howard Schuler was gone completely when this question was out in the air. He turned away from them, taking a moment to haul off and deliver a hard kick to the recliner. It bounced off the wall and rocked on its feet. When Schuler turned back to them, he was enraged.

"Will I *never* escape that fucking accident? Why does everyone think I had something to do with that?" He was screaming now, standing as stiff as a board and yelling pretty much directly into DeMarco's face.

"Mr. Schuler," Kate said softly. "If I were you, I would—"

"I was nowhere near that boy when he was driving. I was not in the passenger seat! I did not reach over and pull the steering wheel into the path of that car and *I did not*—"

Whatever he was going to say next was dissolved in some sort of blind rage. It happened before either Kate or DeMarco knew what was happening because, though he was growing angrier by the moment, he did not look like the sort who would do something stupid.

However, when he uttered that last *I did not*, no other words came out.

Instead, his arms, which had been rigid and trembling up until that point, flew out and struck DeMarco in the chest. It was not a strong attack, but it had been so unexpected that DeMarco could not help but stumble backward. Kate, standing to her left, acted as if she were on some well-oiled spring mechanism and dashed across the three feet that separated her from Schuler. When he saw her coming, he raised his hands into the air and his eyes went wide again. He realized he had screwed up and his brain was trying to quickly catch up to the chain of events.

Kate knew in that moment that she, too, was acting a little harshly. But it had been entirely unexpected—so unexpected that she was also acting on impulse and out of emotion. She swept Schuler's legs out from under him. It was an effective move, sending him to his recliner where he struck the edge, bounced off, and hit the floor.

It must have been embarrassing for him; Kate wasn't sure because she, too, was a little embarrassed. In sweeping him (which had been unnecessary in the first place), she felt something in her lower leg pull. She knew right away it was nothing serious—maybe just some muscle she'd tweaked or something. The sweep had been smooth and natural, but her body had not been prepared for it. Rather than try to get back to her feet, she remained in a half-crouch as DeMarco approached Schuler.

"So that was stupid," DeMarco said, reaching for her cuffs. Kate wasn't sure if DeMarco was talking to her or Schuler.

While DeMarco was busy cuffing Schuler, Kate managed to get to her feet. She tested her weight on the leg and found that, though it was sore, she could still support herself. The only thing that felt slightly off was a slight sense of unbalance in her head. She'd felt this many times before, though, and recognized it as a surge of adrenaline taking one last lap through her nerves before dying out completely.

"I'm sorry," Schuler said. "Really, I didn't mean to! I just... I get so angry whenever people try to blame those four deaths on me..."

"You can explain it all to me down at the precinct," DeMarco said.

"What?" he asked, apparently only then realizing that he had been handcuffed and, as such, placed under arrest. "You have no idea how much shit I've been through over this! There is no proof and I am tired of being the target of this town's witch hunt!"

DeMarco nodded at him and began to read him his rights as she maneuvered him toward the front door. Kate followed behind her and when she did, Kate looked back just once. She gave Kate a grin and a nod of appreciation. Kaye smiled back, doing her best to hide the grimace of pain on her face as she started walking on her injured leg.

Chapter Sixteen

Kate waited for DeMarco to start the interrogation. As it was, she and DeMarco were in the one Harper Hills PD's interrogation room, the room having recently been freed up after Sheriff Gates had let Sammy Curtis go. Now, Howard Schuler sat where Sammy Curtis had sat. He looked terrified and scared. He was still absorbed in the huge mistake he'd made and Kate could pretty much see the rampaging thoughts behind his eyes, wondering just how much trouble he was in.

"Even if you hadn't shoved a federal agent," DeMarco finally said, "you understand that you would have eventually been brought in, right? Or, at the very least, considered a viable suspect."

"I hear you," Schuler said. "But I don't know why."

"It was one thirty when we got to your house and you had been drinking. I am trying to tell myself maybe without the beer in you, you may not have shoved me. How much had you drunk before we got there?"

"Just what you saw on the coffee table. Not a lot."

"Do you usually drink during the early afternoon?"

"Sometimes," he said. "I have sparse work hours on the online school I'm employed by. Sometimes I do drink a lot on my freer days."

"Some might see your drinking as a means of coping with something," DeMarco said. "Maybe three recent murders."

DeMarco said nothing after this, waiting to see if Schuler would try to defend himself. When he didn't, Kate did her best to subtly inject herself into the interrogation. It was quite clear DeMarco had chosen to play the bad cop. That left the kind-hearted and understanding role for Kate.

"What about the questions set you off?" Kate asked.

"It's been almost two years, you know? But everyone in town thinks I gave Jonathan Bowen the alcohol that caused that accident. People call my phone and leave threatening messages. Sometimes they play audio clips of car crashes from movies. Sometimes they'll act as if I can run to the store and grab a six-pack for them." He paused here and Kate grew a little uncomfortable when she saw that he was starting to cry. "Someone... last night, someone called. It was one of the crash recordings and then someone told me I should have been behind that wheel. It's just... I've had enough of it."

Kate and DeMarco remained quiet for a moment longer. DeMarco broke the silence ten seconds later when she asked: "Did you, Mr. Schuler? Were you the one that supplied the alcohol to Jonathan Bowen?"

"No. I swear it."

"How about any other times?" DeMarco leaned in here, as if about to reveal some huge conspiratorial secret. "That is not what this case is about. I can't promise you won't be charged for anything, but that's not what Agent Wise and I are interested in right now. But we need to know because your insider eye to these parties might be exactly what we need."

He started nodding almost right away. It was slow at first, as if his mind wanted to confess but his heart did not. The moment the tears started cascading down his cheeks, though, Kate knew they were on the verge of some sort of revelation.

"Three times," he said. He sniffled back the tears and fought away an emotional breakdown. It took about twenty seconds, but he finally managed to continue on without melting down. "I did it three times. And when I did, it was only beer. At the time, I told myself it was okay because it was beer, not liquor. To my knowledge, there were never any accidents, though one senior did get pulled over later that night and had his license taken away."

"On those three occasions, was Jonathan Bowen ever present?" Kate asked.

"Once that I know of. But that was several months before his accident."

"What about the murder victims?" DeMarco asked. "Vanessa Fenton, Mariah Ogden, and Kayla Peterson... were they ever at any of the parties?"

"Again, Kayla is the only one out of those three that I can specifically remember. And I don't recall her ever being at those parties."

"Have you attended any high school parties since you were fired?" Kate asked.

"Just one. It was pretty clear no one wanted me there. It was one hell of a wake-up call. I just... I don't know. I realized what I had become..."

"There were no confrontations with anyone there?" Kate asked.

"No."

"Mr. Schuler, why do you think you were singled out as a potential guilty party after Jonathan Bowen's accident?"

"I don't know. The only thing I can figure is that at some point, maybe a student did tell their parents they saw me at one of those parties. Or maybe rumors just started to circulate at school and someone else on the faculty heard it. Word got around, but because there was no proof, I don't think anyone dared believe it. But then, when there's an accident as tragic as that one, people will quickly build a rumor up to be the gospel truth. I was an easy target because of the rumors, and that was all she wrote."

"Only they weren't rumors," DeMarco pointed out.

Kate personally felt that Schuler was a dead end. She was sure they could go back and check school records to see if he was lying about not having known Mariah or Vanessa. But if it was proven true, they were doing nothing more than bullying him over his stupid past mistakes. As far as she was concerned, he *did* deserve a bit of bullying, but the phone calls he was getting was taking it a bit too far.

"Rumors, truth, whatever," Schuler said, finally starting to wipe his tears away. "It might sound like I'm trying to play the victim card here, but I don't think the mistakes of my past should result in the rest of my life being ruined. These phone calls and the harassment… it's too much."

"Have you reported it to the police?" Kate asked.

"I tried. But given that everyone in Harper Hills assumed I'm at fault, my complaints weren't taken seriously."

"Any idea who might be making the calls?"

"Students, for the most part. But I've also gotten harassed by some of the women with the local MADD group."

"MADD?" DeMarco asked.

Kate knew what he was talking about and answered for him. "Mothers Against Drunk Driving. And Mr. Schuler, please forgive me for saying this, but that's a pretty serious claim. Do you have proof?"

"One of the women who organizes the meetings essentially chewed me out in the grocery store last year. I honestly thought she was going to start throwing punches. And a few of the phone calls I get are from grown women that don't even try to disguise their voices."

"What's the name of the woman that confronted you in the grocery store?" DeMarco asked.

Kate bit back a frown. She honestly thought speaking to the women at MADD was a waste of time. She didn't see where there was any connection between the murder and a group of mothers who worked together to prevent underage drinking and drinking under the influence. As a matter of fact, she was strongly starting to feel as if they were losing focus and wandering far off their intended path. But she said nothing. This was DeMarco's show and she was curious to see where her younger partner took it.

"Carol Foster," Schuler said. "And I'm sure she'd *love* to tell you all about it."

DeMarco turned to Kate, as if to get her impression. Kate gave a shrug, trying not to seem as if she was disinterested. She thought of the case files, of the three dead girls and the person who had killed them. She felt that a trip to see Carol Foster of MADD was a waste of time.

"Am I still under arrest?" Schuler asked.

DeMarco got to her feet and started for the door. "I won't charge you for shoving me," DeMarco said. "But I'll leave it up to Sheriff Gates how long to keep you here."

Schuler looked like he wanted to argue but decided to drop it just as his mouth opened and he saw the suppressed look on DeMarco's face. Kate gave Schuler one last look as she followed DeMarco out into the hallway.

Demarco sighed almost right away as she turned to Kate. "This MADD thing... you think it's a stretch?"

Kate smiled. "Was it that obvious?"

"A little. But you know... we know that Vanessa Fenton did mushrooms the night she died. If she does things like that, I wonder if she had been drinking."

"What if she had?"

"Well, it makes me wonder if they had *all* been drinking."

"What if they had? It's a small town. Underage drinking is probably, sadly, the norm."

"But at least it would be a link. And if it *is* a link, what group do you think might have more information about local underage drinking and those involved than the local chapter of Mothers Against Drunk Driving?"

Kate couldn't help but smile. She thought she might have eventually gotten there, but DeMarco had beaten her to it.

All right, old lady, Kate thought to herself. *You pulled a muscle sweeping a guy that weighs under two hundred pounds and you were slow to the jump on what now looks like a pretty logical next step. This seems to be a young woman's game now and you need to catch the hell up. Or do you even want to?*

She didn't dare search for an answer. Instead, she walked down the hall in search of Sheriff Gates to ask him for the number to the medical examiner.

Chapter Seventeen

The medical examiner was an older gentleman named Carl Maxwell. He had a soothing voice which was almost morbid, considering what he did for a living. When Kate spoke with him, she could easily imagine him recording one of those calming yoga narrations to help people focus.

"The toxicology reports revealed that only one of the victims was intoxicated at the time of their death," Maxwell said. "That was Mariah Ogden. Kayla Peterson had some alcohol in her system, not enough for me to think she would have been drunk. She might have had a total of two beers if I had to guess."

"And what about Vanessa Fenton?"

"Her blood levels were all over the place. I'm fairly certain she was doing a drug of some kind, but I saw no traces of alcohol."

"The abnormalities in her blood levels... do you think they would be indicative of mushrooms or some other psychedelic?"

"Let's see," Maxwell said. Kate could hear him typing something into a computer and then humming to himself. About fifteen seconds later he made an "a-ha" noise. "Yes, I think that would be a suitable explanation. Because we just got the body recently, a more conclusive study should be completed sometime tonight."

Kate almost ended it on that note, but felt a link right there, within her grasp. It might be a stretch, but certainly worth checking out.

"Mr. Maxwell, is there any way you could rush those results? It might be very important to find out if Vanessa was drinking."

"Of course. I'll let you know as soon as I find out."

Kate ended the call, knowing they could simply go back to Jenna and ask. She had, after all, confessed to using the mushrooms. But as far as Kate was concerned, a drug test of Venessa's blood would trump Jenna's word easily. If she had to wait a bit rather than retreading old ground, that was fine with her.

Besides, if her link was right and all three girls had been drinking on the night they were killed, it suddenly made another lead they had stumbled upon seem all the more promising.

She walked back to their makeshift office and happened to find DeMarco standing in the doorway to Gates's office. She was looking over a sheet of paper with numbers and graphs on it.

"What's that?" Kate asked.

"Sheriff Gates was kind enough to find a record that the local MADD chapter sent in a few weeks after the Jonathan Bowen accident," DeMarco said, handing it over to her. Inside the office, sitting at his desk, Gates looked a little uneasy.

Kate looked at the paper as Gates explained the results. "Some of the women with MADD worked with us to find the number of traffic accidents involving not only drunk driving, but specifically when the drivers were under twenty-one years of age. As you can see, the results *are* a little staggering."

"They usually are," Kate said. "This is from two years ago, right?"

"That's right."

"Anything more recent? Maybe to show newer trends and results?"

Gates shook his head and frowned. "There's no way to say this without sounding like I take issue with MADD—and please, God knows that I have no problems with the organization. In some larger cities and towns, the work they do is actually pretty amazing. But here in Harper Hills, not so much. They like to raise hell to the point where it becomes almost like a public shaming of the parents that aren't aware their kids are drinking. So when these results came out and were even published in the local paper, they sort of went quiet afterwards."

"So, sort of like they had made their point and then disappeared into the woodwork?" DeMarco asked.

Gates chuckled and said, "You said it, not me."

"Who provided you with this report?" Kate asked, stepping into the office and placing the sheet on his desk.

"Carol Foster."

"That's the woman that berated Schuler in the grocery store, right?"

"The same."

DeMarco grinned at her and folded her arms in a playful sort of posture. "You want to tell me your theory in private or do you want Gates to see how your mind works?"

Kate knew it was meant as a compliment, but for some reason, she felt almost outed. Still, she had no problem letting them know where her mind was headed.

"We've got three underage girls, recent high school graduates, and the only clear link we have between them is that they were drinking the night they died. The ME said there's no clear proof that Vanessa Fenton had been drinking, but I'm going to venture a guess and say that if they were doing 'shrooms and hanging out at a place Jenna Marshall's parents did not want her to be, I don't think it's a stretch to think that Vanessa was drinking."

"So you think... what?" Gates said. "That the killer is targeting high school graduates that are not yet twenty-one, and are drinking?"

"It fits all the pieces we have right now. And while it doesn't seem to make much sense on its face, I think it's a good place to start looking."

"I can go along with that," DeMarco said. "It does, of course, beg the question why the killer targeted Vanessa and not Jenna. They'd been together all day, so he had his pick last night, or so it seems."

"Not if Vanessa's car was at Jenna's house," Kate pointed out. "If they were both together, it would have been riskier. I think he followed Vanessa from Jenna's house. Or maybe he even had deeper knowledge than that. Maybe he knew when Vanessa would be heading home."

"But how?"

"How would he know they had been drinking at all?" Kate asked.

"Because he had probably seen them that some point that night," Gates offered.

"Most likely," Kate agreed.

DeMarco looked to Gates and asked: "How hard would it be for you to get together a list of all DUIs in the area over the last two or three years?"

"Not long. And you'd be surprised... it's not too long of a list. But... yeah. It's mostly going to be people between the ages of sixteen and twenty-five or so."

"Thanks," DeMarco said. She then nodded toward the sheet of paper Kate had placed back on Gates's desk. "In the meantime, what do you say we go meet with Carol Foster?"

"You won't have a hard time finding her either," Gates said. "Her and some of her friends get together once a week at Esther's Place on Monday afternoons. Sort of a MADD meeting, I guess, though I'd bet it's really just an opportunity to gossip."

"What time?" Kate asked.

"Five o'clock. Like clockwork."

Kate checked her watch and saw that it had somehow already come to be four o'clock. She grinned, as a meeting with Carol Foster and her friends seemed to be written in the stars.

"Esther's Place seems to be the only place to get together for dinner and drinks in town," DeMarco said. "Is it the hotbed for police calls on the weekend?"

"Not as many as you'd think. It used to have a pretty bad reputation for serving underage kids, but that got cleaned up several years ago. Now the owners are professional and do everything they can do curb underage drinking."

"You know this for certain?"

"I do. I swing by there at least three times a month unexpectedly. They don't appreciate it, but they understand and are hospitable about it."

"You trust the establishment?" Kate asked.

"Yes. Plus, this is a small town. Every bartender is going to know just about everyone's face. That eliminates any so-called accidents where a bartender might forget to card someone on a busy night."

"This will be our second visit since we arrived," Kate said with a laugh. "If we keep showing up, they'll know our faces, too."

⚜ ⚜ ⚜

It was almost exactly the same as when they had met with Kayla Peterson's friends, right down to the same booth. Only now, the women sitting at the table were about twenty-five years older and had drinks in front of them. *Sadly ironic,* Kate thought as she sat down and introductions were made.

Gates had done them the favor of calling Carol Foster to let her know that the agents would be arriving. According to Gates, she had been ecstatic about the news, pleased to know that finally someone seemed to be taking the underage drinking in this town seriously. When Carol shook Kate's hand as she and

DeMarco sat down, Kate instantly got a bad vibe from the woman. Maybe it was her smile or the fact that the head of the local MADD chapter was having a cocktail out in the open at five in the afternoon—she wasn't sure.

"Sheriff Gates told me you two are in town to try to figure out who has been killing these beautiful young women," Carol said.

"We are," Kate said.

"So—and please forgive me for saying so—it confuses me as to why you'd need to speak to us."

Us consisted of Carol and two other women. The others had introduced themselves as Paulette Manning and Ava Fears. Paulette looked to be pushing fifty and had one of those humorless smiles that always seemed to be painted on the faces of those seeking approval. Ava looked to the exact opposite. She was clearly uneasy with the meeting, looking sheepishly at the agents from under a curtain of jet black bangs.

"One of the suspects we were questioning mentioned your name. Said you laid into him in the middle of a grocery store because you thought he had been supplying underage kids with alcohol."

"I suppose that was Howard Schuler," Carol said. "I'm sure there are a few others in Harper Hills, but he was the most prominent on our list because of his position at the high school." She chuckled here and then asked: "Was he trying to throw me under the bus?"

"No, nothing like that. He was telling us how everyone blamed him for the accident that took the life of four people, included a teenager and a baby."

"Oh, it *was* his fault," Paulette chimed in.

"Do you have proof of that?" DeMarco asked.

"No, but everyone knows he—"

"Everyone knowing something does not make it proof," DeMarco snapped. She looked back to Carol and added, "And it certainly doesn't give you permission to berate someone in the middle of a public place. You are trying to lay a *very* serious crime and consequence at his feet."

There was silence among them for a moment as they all started to understand that a meeting that had begun as leisurely had now become something very different.

"I'm sorry," Carol said. "What, exactly, did you need from us?"

Kate sized Carol up as a silence fell among the table. Carol was a pretty woman, though not what some men would consider *hot.* She had a figure that spoke of some sort of physicality, though not quite of dieting and heavy self-care. And even though she and DeMarco were only here to gather information about other potential individuals similar to Schuler, Carol was getting defensive—which didn't say much for her character.

"We saw your reports from around the time after Jonathan Bowen's accident," Kate said. "It was very well put together. Have you continued with the study?"

"No. Those numbers were circulated around the schools. I think we did our part."

"Did you, though?" Kate asked. She could feel herself getting irritated. She was starting to get a feel for Carol Foster. She was a holier-than-thou type, quick to demonize others so she could look like a hero. Sure, there was no doubt that Howard Schuler had made mistakes and was not the most reliable or honorable man in town. But he would also never be able to escape the shadow of his mistakes if people like Carol Foster kept circulating old rumors just to heighten her throne.

"What's that supposed to mean?" Paulette asked. Beside her, Ava looked as if she might be looking for any excuse to just get out of there.

"Well, we're now looking into three murders and it looks like each victim may have been inebriated. So maybe your little efforts aren't doing what you were hoping."

"If you think—"

"Wait," DeMarco said, interrupting Carol.

Kate sensed the frustration in that single word. She realized that she had not only gotten rather personal with Carol, but had also revealed a few details of the case that had no business going public. Her emotions were clearly getting the better of her.

"I believe what my partner meant to say," DeMarco went on, "is that it makes little sense to put so much effort into a report like that and then not really put anything new out in the years that follow just because you feel you successfully smeared the person you thought might be responsible for that tragic accident."

"That was not my intention," Carol said.

Kate nearly started to speak again but decided against it. She sat back in the seat, making sure to bite her tongue.

"We're honestly not even here to argue that point," DeMarco said. "We're here because we thought that, being the MADD lead for the area, you might know some names of people that are similar to Howard Schuler. Is there anyone else that you know of that might fit his description?"

Carol looked confused, yet she also turned her attention to Paulette and Ava. She did not do this as if looking for help in answering the question. Instead, she was giving her friends disbelieving looks. She was finding it hard to believe that Kate and DeMarco had come to them for this sort of help.

"What's wrong?" Kate asked. She saw DeMarco look at her from the left, maybe giving her a let's-pump-the-brakes sort of stare. But she ignored it.

"Nothing is wrong."

"Ms. Foster, what do you do for a living?"

Carol cocked her head, trying to understand why the question was being asked. Slowly, though, she answered. "I'm a physical trainer."

"In your line of work, do you ever meet with people that you absolutely trust? Would you trust all of your clients with your life?"

"Maybe one or two. But I don't know the others well enough to make that sort of choice. I'm sorry . . . what the hell are you getting at?"

"Three girls are dead in less than a week. Six parents are in mourning. We're asking you a very simple question and you seem to be troubled by that. Can I ask why?"

"You already questioned Schuler, right? If you want to know who is killing these young women, he's your best bet. He's not exactly known for hanging with the right crowds and—"

"I don't need you to tell me how to do my job," Kate said. Her voice was loud—louder than she had intended—and she realized that if this carried on the way it was, she was going to end up causing a scene.

"I'm doing no such thing," Carol said. "You've arrested Howard Schuler, right? If you ask me, you're doing a damn fine job."

Kate was fuming and, for a moment, thought she was going to have to excuse herself outside before she said something totally unprofessional. And the real hell of it was that she had no idea why she was so irate.

Thankfully, DeMarco stepped in and kept her from saying anything. "Could you three ladies account for your whereabouts on any night I ask about over the past week?"

She got three quick nods in response; Carol looked to her friends once more but the cockiness was gone. She was now taken aback and, Kate was happy to see, a little scared.

"Wednesday night, Saturday night, and last night," DeMarco said. "I need to know where you all were between the hours of ten and six."

"At night?" Ava asked. "At home. I go to sleep at ten."

"I was at home, too," Carol said. "My husband will attest to that. But still, if you're insinuating that one of us—"

DeMarco held a hand up, silencing her as Paulette answered. "I was at home as well. Though, on Wednesday night, I did have to pick my daughter up from cheerleading practice at the high school and I did not get back home until ten thirty or so."

"You're all married?" DeMarco asked. "With husbands that can back this up?"

Again, they got three nods in response.

"I'll ask again, and then we're done here," DeMarco asked. "Can none of you think of anyone else that may have made some of the same mistakes as Howard Schuler?"

There was a moment of silence before Paulette spoke up. "No. Honestly, Schuler was the only man I ever heard of that was mixing in with the younger crowd. And you're right . . . there is no proof. Just stories. But I can't think of anyone else."

"Same," Carol said, clearly done with the conversation. "It's a small town. If anyone was actively giving alcohol to minors, we'd hear about it. And that's why I said I'm glad you arrested Schuler. It's been a long time coming."

DeMarco waited a moment, making sure to look at each woman before she got to her feet. When she finally did get up, she gave the trio of women a simple wave of the hand as she left the table. Kate followed behind her, not bothering to look back. She'd encountered countless women like Carol Foster in her thirty-plus years as an agent—and if Carol Foster was the last of them, Kate did not want to give the woman the satisfaction of getting any more of her attention.

Chapter Eighteen

They left Esther's Place and found a small Italian restaurant at the edge of town. Over pizza and beer, they looked through the scant case files and went through the case detail by detail. Kate enjoyed it very much. Yes, it was work and it was trying to put a case together, but it was also very close to what some might consider hanging out. They ate and drank as night fell on Harper Hills outside. Kate looked out there, wondering if the killer was peering into that same coming darkness, making plans for another death.

"Carol Foster seemed hell bent on making sure we thought Howard Schuler is just a terrible human being, didn't she?" DeMarco said.

"She did," Kate agreed. "And it makes me wonder why she wants us to look so closely at him. I'm fairly certain just based on her attitude that it wasn't for the best interest of the case."

"You think she might be trying to shrug attention off of her? In this town, it seems to have worked. The stuff Gates had to say, as well as Principal Robinson . . . Howard Schuler may as well be a leper."

Kate bit off a slice of pizza, considering it. "And maybe that could drive him to kill the young women," she offered. "Maybe he just had enough and, because people think he purchased the alcohol responsible for that terrible accident, decided to go after underage drinkers. The motive would be there, but . . ."

"But he doesn't seem like a killer," DeMarco finished.

"Exactly. Of course, we still need to make absolutely sure he's free to go, but I doubt he killed them."

"However, it does make you wonder about the timing. The killer seemed to have waited for Thanksgiving break. He knew these girls would be home and apparently knew they would be drinking."

"And by that standard, Schuler *would* fit the description. It's a small town and he has a past of partying with young kids. Who would know better than him which girls are being irresponsible?"

"It's certainly a lot of unanswered questions," DeMarco said. "And if you don't mind my asking... is that why you seem to be getting so upset?"

"What do y—"

"Oh, Kate, please don't even try that. I've never seen you react to someone the way you did with Carol Foster. Sure, she wasn't very pleasant to be around, but you were verging on unprofessional."

"I know. I let her get under my skin. There's no excuse."

"You're right." She seemed irritated still, but decided to let it go. "I think we need to hold on to Schuler, primarily for all of the reasons we just listed."

"You really think it's him?" Kate asked.

"I think he has the motive and knowledge of most of the student body from the high school over the last several years. I'm not willing to say he's innocent just because he shows signs of regret for his past. If he's really endured that much teasing and abuse over the last few years, who knows what he'd be capable of."

Kate wanted to argue but couldn't in that moment. DeMarco had a solid argument and, honestly, one that Kate would have stood by several years ago. But she'd seen enough killers—as well as enough wrongfully accused suspects—to know when her initial read on someone was accurate. She felt it with Howard Schuler, and everything in her told her that he was not a killer. They had disagreed on the perceived innocence of a suspect before, but Kate thought this one might have the potential to truly divide them.

As they finished eating, storing the leftover pizza in to-go boxes, Kate felt her phone vibrating in her pocket. She didn't even bother checking the ID as she and DeMarco headed for the door.

"This Agent Wise."

"Agent Wise, this is Carl Maxwell, the county's medical examiner. I've got some results for you."

"Great," Kate said. She stopped before exiting, wanting to focus solely on what he had to say.

"First of all, I can indeed confirm that Vanessa Fenton also had traces of alcohol in her bloodstream; they were simply a little harder to find because of the strange nature of the mushrooms she had also ingested. So there's the first link: all three of the victims had been drinking on the night they were killed."

"You said that was the *first* link. Did you find something else?"

"We think we did. As you know, all three women were strangled. There are a few perfect shapes of fingers bruises, though we can't use them as identifiers. However, a closer analysis shows that the primary way the women were strangled was with some sort of a rope or band of some kind. We just got some lab results back from potential fibers found on all three women. Some of the fibers were found in their hair, some on their clothes, and all three had the fibers present on their necks."

"What sort of fibers are we talking about?"

"That's just it. We don't know for sure. We do have some characteristic, though. It appears that whatever was used to strangle these women was made of a synthetic material, some sort of rayon. It had a goldish sort of color to it and at least one other—a second color that appears to either be a red or maroon. We thought it might be blood at first, but it seems to be dyed right into the fibers."

"That's a pretty big step forward," Kate said.

"Any idea where it might all point?"

"Not yet. But this could potentially be a big help. Thanks, Mr. Maxwell."

She ended the call and found DeMarco standing beside her, wanting an update. Kate filled her in as they exited the restaurant and headed for the car. As DeMarco cranked the engine to life, a thoughtful look crossed her face.

"Think you got something?" Kate asked.

"Not sure. But when we met with Principal Robinson, do you remember what she was wearing?"

Kate had to think about it for a moment, but slowly started to nod. "She was wearing a Stateside High windbreaker." And then, right behind it came another realization. "The school colors are maroon and gold."

"I think it fits too well to be a coincidence, don't you?" DeMarco asked.

"Absolutely. But it still doesn't tell us what the killer is using to strangle the women with."

"Maybe not, but it does tell us the killer owns at least a few things with the Stateside High logo. I think it narrows out search down to either current or recent students, or even employees. And that would include former employees, like Howard Schuler."

Again, DeMarco had a good point but even with this new bit of information, Kate found it hard to picture Schuler as the killer.

"I think we need to get a list of current or former employees with any black marks on their record," Kate said. "Even if nothing turns up, we might be able to get some more under-the-table information on Schuler."

"Let's get that going, then," DeMarco said, pulling out onto the road and pointing the car back toward the police station.

"It does make you wonder, doesn't it?" Kate said.

"Wonder what, exactly?"

"Hypothetically, let's say there *is* some other teacher or faculty member was that doing the same unprofessional things as Schuler. They'd probably be tight, right? Probably friends that would have each other's back."

"Probably. It would make sense."

"I'm not sure where I'm trying to go with it," she said. "It's just always blown my mind that in little towns like this, secret are sometimes easier to keep than they are in bigger cities."

"Which do you prefer?" DeMarco asked. "Cases in bigger cities or smaller ones?"

"Honestly? Bigger ones. In bigger cities, people tend to be more forthcoming with gossip. Always wanting to see someone get nailed for something. In smaller towns, people keep their secrets close and the isolation makes it easier for them. You?"

DeMarco shrugged. "I don't know yet. I'm still learning. And learning from the very best, I might add."

Kate wasn't sure what to say, as she had never been great at receiving flattery. She supposed it was one of the reasons she'd had such a hard time dealing with the whole Miracle Mom nonsense. It was unwanted attention that she honestly didn't deserve. She had sex as a fifty-six-year-old and got pregnant. People did it all the time . . . just not at her age.

Besides, at the moment, she didn't feel like a Miracle Mom. If anything, she felt like a pretty bad mother, leaving both of her children behind without much of an explanation. Melissa was used to it and Michael would have no idea she was even gone, probably.

Remember when you used to thrive on making excuses like that?

The thought caused her to turn her head to the right, staring out the window as the night rolled by, the small town flickering past in a series of dark shapes that hid innumerable secrets.

Chapter Nineteen

After spending an hour at the police department, Kate and DeMarco called it a day and headed to their hotel. It was 9:04 when Kate stepped into her room and started to set up a workstation on the little table by the bed. Gates and a few other officers had worked quickly and efficiently to get them any records they had on current and former Stateside High employees and, as Kate had suspected, there wasn't much to go on.

Kate looked over the copied records, taking notes and looking for links and obvious connections. The only alarming file Gates had provided concerned a math teacher who, six years ago, openly quit his job because he had developed romantic feelings for an eleventh grader. Two weeks later, he had attempted to kill himself in the bathtub. He was later arrested for breaking the guidelines of a restraining order not once, not twice, but three different times. An odd little twist to the story was that after that student graduated, she visited him in prison at least once a month.

It had absolutely nothing to do with their case, but was a stark reminder that you couldn't underestimate the capacity in people to hide secrets or, even worse, to openly embrace their flaws and act out on them. She searched for connections between this teacher and any of the others in the short list Gates had given them, but found nothing. It did, however, make her think of the conversation she and DeMarco had shared in the car about the hypothetical situation of Howard Schuler having a friend or two that were into the same sorts of bad habits.

She was just about to take another look at Schuler's history when her phone rang. When she saw that it was Allen, her heart surged a bit in her chest. She answered it right away with a cheerful "Hey, you."

"Hey. I waited until now to call because I wanted to make sure you were off the clock."

"I am. How are you holding up?"

"Michael and I are doing pretty good. He got a little fussier than usual today but I think that's just because he senses something different. The pretty lady isn't here and I don't think he quite understands what going on."

"I know. I'm sorry."

"I didn't mean for that come off as accusing. Just thought you might want to know that your boy misses you."

"I miss him, too. And you as well."

"Likewise. Listen, there's no easy way to say this, but I think there's going to need to be some sort of conversation between us and Melissa when you're done with this case."

"Why is that? Is everything okay?"

"Overall, yes. But she came by today just to visit. Had Michelle with her and was happy to see Michael. But apparently, you didn't let her know you were taking this case. When I told her the news, she was surprised at first and then . . . well, then she was *pissed*."

"I honestly didn't think I needed to tell her. This was supposed to be an easy case and—"

"Well, the ridiculous thing is that she tried to take it out on me. She asked me how in the hell I could let you go back to work. Kate, I'd never seen her like that before. She was crying and said it's just like when she was younger. She's afraid you're going to neglect Michael."

"Of course I'm not going to . . ."

She stopped herself here, sensing where the conversation was going and how it might take a terrible turn.

"How long did she stay?" Kate asked.

"Maybe fifteen minutes. She ranted for a bit and then left."

"I suppose I should talk to her."

"If you can, I'd do it now. I understand her frustration, but she was pretty damned rude to me. I also didn't appreciate her screaming in front of Michael."

"Allen, this is all going to be over soon. I feel pretty confident about that. But as I said before, I can't just bail on this case right in the middle of it."

He let out a sigh and then gave an exasperated chuckle. "I'll buy it a bit longer, so you don't need to sell it to me. Just call your daughter, will you?"

"Allen . . ."

"It's okay. We're good. I'll talk to you later. Much love."

"Damn it, wait a minute!"

She had nearly yelled this at him. She shuddered when it was out, ashamed that she had lost control. When Allen responded, his voice was thick with an anger she had not heard from him before.

"What?"

"I didn't mean for any of this to happen. I can't . . . I can't walk away from this case now. I can't be there to be the referee for fights between you and her."

"Well, that's the thing, Kate. Melissa and I have never had words before. I apologize if this is stepping over some imaginary line, but she is expecting me to do something that her father was never able to do and I can't handle that weight. I can't rein you in. I can't make you stop. And she knows she can't, either. She can't handle that, Kate. Like I said, you just need to talk to her."

"I know. And I'm sorry for screaming. Really. I don't know what the hell is wrong with me."

The other end of the line was silent for a moment until Allen said: "Let's you and I try to figure that out when you get home. You just be safe out there and make sure you *do* make it back home."

He hung up before she could respond. She gripped the phone tightly, wanting to feel angry and, more than that, wanting to feel justified in that anger. But, in the same way she was beginning to understand that DeMarco's personality was changing, she also had to understand that Allen and Melissa were also changing. They knew she needed to stop and felt helpless to say much of anything. Melissa was afraid because she did not want to relive her childhood, having her mother never be there for her. And Allen was still trying to find his place in this strange little family unit with a fifty-seven-year-old mother and retirement just up ahead.

And they were right. That was the hardest thing to accept. Even now, knowing that there was at the very least one more day left in this case—and potentially many more—she felt more than ever that the legitimate end of her career was on the horizon; if not after this case, then maybe the one after that or the one after that. And because of this, she could not give up. Not because Melissa was mad, not because Allen was frustrated, and not because there seemed to be some sort of growing tension between her and DeMarco.

No, she needed to wrap this case for her own reward. After thirty-three years as an agent, she would not throw in the towel on a case she felt was very likely her last.

With a heavy heart, she called Melissa. She answered almost right away and there was instantly venom in her voice. "Did Allen tell on me?"

"He did."

"Perfect. Like I'm some sort of child."

"From what I hear, you threw a temper tantrum as if you *are* a child."

"At least I can let go of things. Jesus, Mom, how important is that job to you? Is your entire identity so wrapped up in it that you're blind to any sort of life outside of it?"

Kate opened her mouth to respond but found that she could not form the words. As sad as it sounded, Melissa had pretty much summed up the problem that had plagued most of their relationship. Work had always come first. Solving cases and working toward justice had always trumped anything at home. It hurt to admit it, but there it was, plain and simple.

"Maybe," Kate finally said. She wanted to add that she was all but certain this case would be her last, but didn't bother. Melissa had heard that one before and would not believe her until it was being lived out.

"Mom... you've got to stop. I know you're feeling like a rock star because you somehow had a baby at your age, but you've got to quit. Fifty-seven, Mom. You're fifty-seven and a grandmother and, as odd as it sounds, a *new mom.* What the hell are you doing?"

The answer was: *the only thing I was really any good at.* But she could not bring herself to admit this to her daughter.

"Why were you so hard on Allen? He's not responsible for my decisions."

"No, but he apparently didn't put up much of a fight. He knows as well as I do that you're only clinging to this job because you're stubborn and can't see yourself without it. He could have tried harder to talk you out of it."

"He wants to see me happy," Kate said.

"Oh, I know that for a fact. That man is stupid in love with you. But don't you want to see *him* happy? Mom, don't you want your new son to be happy?"

"Of course."

"Then show them. Prove it."

Kate didn't realize she was pacing until she found herself at the window, looking out to the darkened parking lot. She rarely paced, only resorting to the habit when she was either deep in thought or anxious about something.

"I'm getting there," was all she could say.

"You have to do better than that, Mom."

Kate was looking out the window, her fingers pulling the curtains lightly to the side. The little tassels of silk that tied the curtains together brushed her arm. When she pushed one of them to the side, her mind seemed to freeze for a moment. There was something there, some link, some thought…

"Melissa, I need to go, okay?"

"Seriously, Mom?"

"Yes, seriously. If you want me working this out, I need to be present right here, where I am right now. And in the meantime, you need to call Allen and apologize."

"Are you kidding?"

"No, I'm not," she said. She fingered the silk tassel, her mind latching on to the thought that had come to her before it had a chance to slip through the cracks. "And just so you know, yes, I'm aware of how stubborn and selfish I seem right now. But you have to trust me when I tell you that it's almost over."

"Mom…"

"Really, Melissa. I have to go now. Call Allen. I love you."

"Love you, too."

The closing comment meant everything to Kate. When Melissa was really angry, she withheld those words as some sort of stubborn punishment. It's why Kate felt almost relieved when she ended the call and turned all of her attention to the ribbon along the edges of the curtain.

The little tie-tassels weren't really silk; they just looked like it. It reminded Kate of some other material she had seen before, something she could not quite grasp.

Not until she pictured the navy blue ribbons as being colored in gold and marron.

She saw it then—she saw that the tassels that were used to tie the curtains together were made of pretty much the same rayon-based material as the tassels on the backs of graduation caps. She heard Carl Maxwell in the back of her head, telling her that it appeared the victims had all been strangled with some sort of cord or strap that looked to be made of rayon or a similar material. And the strap or whatever was being used had left behind fibers that were gold and maroon in color—the school colors of Stateside High.

It could be the tassels and cord from the back of a graduation cap, Kate thought. *But what does it mean?*

Her mind seemed to be on fire with theories and ideas. She checked the clock and saw that it was 9:35, perhaps too late to call people at home.

But she had to act quickly. She felt like she was on to something significant—so significant that she was willing to look past social niceties. With her notions and gut instinct pushing her, Kate picked up her phone and started to place a few calls.

Chapter Twenty

Principal Robinson sounded understandably irritated to be bothered at 9:35 at night. But when Kate told her who she was, Robinson seemed to be more agreeable. She sounded tired and, if Kate was hearing the woman's tone right, a bit worried as well.

"I'm sorry if I woke you or disturbed your home life in any way," Kate said. "But I'm pursuing a line of thought and I need you to confirm something for me before I get too deep into it."

"It's fine. What can I do for you, Agent Wise?"

"When Agent DeMarco and I met with you, you were wearing a windbreaker with your school's logo on it. The windbreaker was maroon and gold if my memory serves correct. Are those the official school colors for Stateside High?"

"Yes, they are."

"So I assume those would be the colors on most school merchandise and materials for Spirit Week and that sort of thing."

"Yes, that is correct. Some people think it's a little too close to the colors of the Washington Redskins, which is a nightmare being this close to Panther country." She chuckled here, but dryly. It was clear she had made this joke before.

"What about at graduation, with cap and gowns?"

"Well, the yellow or gold makes for a terrible color for a graduation robe," Robinson said. "So we offer the students a choice of maroon or traditional black."

"And what about the hats? Are the tassels maroon and gold?"

"They are. And maybe I'm a little too sentimental, but seeing that gold and maroon going up in the air and sort of fluttering around when they toss their caps still gives me chills."

It gave Kate chills, too.

But for an entirely different reason.

⚜ ⚜ ⚜

The next call she made was to the Harper Hills police station. She placed the call on speaker mode as she got dressed to head back out. The phone was answered by an older-sounding man Kate assumed was working the dispatch desk.

"Is Sheriff Gates there by any chance?" she asked.

"No, I'm afraid not," the man said. "Can I ask who is calling?"

"This is Agent Kate Wise with the FBI. My partner and I have been working with him."

"Oh yes, of course. The sheriff is home for the night, but Officer Smith is still here if you'd like to speak with him."

Kate was placed on hold and transferred over. Smith picked the call up less than ten seconds later. "Everything okay, Agent?"

"Yes, I'm fine, but I'm heading back to the station. I'll be there in about fifteen minutes. Do you think you could start digging up some information for me?"

"Anything you need."

"I know it's going to be a tall order and we probably can't get a complete list until tomorrow, but I need a list of high school dropouts in the area over the past decade or so. I feel certain Principal Robinson would help. Is that something we can start on effectively tonight?"

"That's a tricky one, but I'll see what I can do."

"Thanks, Officer Smith. Oh . . . and another thing. It might seem like an odd question, but when did you graduate high school?"

"Oh gosh, that's been twenty years ago. Actually, twenty-one. Why do you ask?"

"Is there anybody on the force who may have graduated more recently?"

"There's a guy that just joined last year. He's twenty-five years old, so he would have graduated . . . .what? About seven years ago. You looking for anything in particular?"

"A graduation cap."

"Oh," Smith said, just as confused as when he had been asked for a list of dropouts. "Well, that's another strange one, but I'll see what we can do for you."

She ended the call, slipped on her shoes, and headed out. She walked down the little breezeway to the room next door. She knew DeMarco wouldn't be asleep yet so had no qualms about knocking on the door. Ten seconds after knocking, there was still no answer so she knocked again, a little more insistent this time. Again, there was no answer. She looked into the window and though the curtains were drawn, she could tell that the lights were out.

Strange, Kate thought. She then walked to the parking lot and saw that their car was still parked there. Confused, Kate pulled out her cell phone and called DeMarco's number. It rang several times and then went to voicemail.

Kate figured DeMarco could have gone to sleep early and was just refusing to come to the door or answer her phone. None of that *seemed* like DeMarco, though.

Maybe she went back to the station, too, Kate thought. *If she did, maybe she was courteous in leaving me the car and taking a cab.*

It seemed like a flimsy explanation, but it was the only thing that made sense. With a final look back to the window to DeMarco's room, Kate got into the car and pulled out of the parking lot.

Chapter Twenty One

Darla Dowdy blew a plume of smoke out of her car window as she watched the little pickup truck roll in beside her car. She was parked on the side aisle of the Quick Stop parking lot, where she had once come to smoke with friends in high school. The cold November air coming in through the window actually felt good. It was the one pleasant thing she had endured tonight. If she was being honest, it was the one pleasant thing she'd experienced since coming home four days ago for her fall break.

She'd been a year behind everyone in high school—not grade wise, but age wise. She'd always been a year younger than everyone, having a December birthday So when she graduated at seventeen, most of her friends had been eighteen. And now, three years later, she was the sole twenty-year-old remaining in her original circle of friends. It was a circle that had gotten smaller after she had left for college and even smaller now that everyone else was of drinking age.

She watched as the driver of the truck rolled down his window. He was a scuzzy-looking guy as far as Darla was concerned but probably a "catch" in the eyes of the local idiot women here in town.

Darla rolled her window down a bit more to speak with him. She was pretty sure she recognized his face—which wasn't really saying much in a town as small as Harper Hills.

"Hey there, sweetness," he said.

She rolled her eyes. "Nope. Don't even try it. I do have to say, though . . . you're like clockwork."

"How's that?"

"You're that guy, you know?"

"No, I don't."

"Oh, I think you do." As she spoke to him, Darla was really concerned about this current plan of hers. But all of her friends had essentially cut her out. They were all in Charlotte, hitting up some clubs. They could do that because they were twenty-one and that apparently made them much more sophisticated than her. It angered her more than she cared to admit. It made her want to drink, too. She'd even tried getting a few drinks at the bowling alley earlier, and they'd carder her and turned her away. She almost hoped that bit of information made it back to her mother. She'd have an absolute fit.

"Tell me, then," the guy said.

"You're the guy that buys cigarettes and beer for kids under twenty-one. You know, they say you come by here three times a night most weekends, and every night around closing. Just to see if anyone needs your services."

"I do what I can," he said with a shrug. "What can I do for you, sweetness?"

"You can stop calling me sweetness, first of all. And after that, just a six-pack." She paused here and sighed. "Fuck it. A twelve-pack."

"Any certain kind?"

"Nothing with the word Lite in it."

"Twenty-five bucks," he said.

She knew it was more than a twelve-pack cost, but she also knew he charged for taking the risk. She'd been hearing about this guy for about two years now, and wondered how much he made off of kids. She also wondered how young he was willing to go. She thought of this cretin buying beer for thirteen-year-olds and almost changed her mind. But she was depressed and, as much as she hated to admit it, just wanted to get drunk by herself. In her mind, it was the best sort of therapy. She'd get drunk alone at her parents' house, watching TV and texting college friends. Her folks were away to visit some extended family for an early Thanksgiving get-together. Darla had come home early, thinking she could hang with her friends at her parents' place, but her asshole friends had opted for a club over an hour and a half away instead. So stupid.

It made her think drinking alone would be preferable. It sounded much better than what her other friends were doing, hitting up clubs in Charlotte and, in the case of one of those so-called friends, probably getting some sort of STD in the men's bathroom. Or (and she felt very bad to even think such a thing) maybe they'd get pulled over and whoever was driving would have to take a breathalyzer and fail it. Happy Thanksgiving, bitches.

She fished twenty-five bucks out of her purse and handed it through the window. As she did, though, the lights to the Quick Stop shut off. She looked to the digital clock on her console and cursed. Somehow, it had already come to be ten o'clock.

"Are they seriously closed?"

He looked just as surprised as she was, but it was a look that was quickly replaced by a terrible shit-eating grin. "Yeah, that sucks."

"Well, I guess we're done here," Darla said.

"How bad do you want it?" the guy asked, clearly amused by the double entendre.

"Oh, you're priceless." She was about to leave right then and there but her desperation was just that strong. Was she really that weak and hopeless?

Yes. Apparently, she was. "You got other ideas?"

"Yeah. The Kroger in Glensville is open twenty-four hours and sells booze until midnight."

"You expect me to follow you to Glensville?"

"You don't have to. I'll go get it. There are some kids there I usually help out, too. The price will go up, though. Gas and all."

"Of course it will."

"You know, we don't have to exchange money for it at all. There are other ways you could pay."

He gave her a smoldering look that she assumed was supposed to make her melt. It did not. What it did was make her want to punch him. "No, I'm good. Cash is fine."

"Forty bucks."

"That's extortion."

"You could just sleep with me. Or just oral would be good."

"Forty it is. Do I just meet you here?"

"Not after hours," he said. "That's way too easy for the cops. You tell me where to meet you and I'll bring it to you."

"I don't think so."

"You said you heard about me, right? I've been doing this a while, you know? I don't get that sort of reputation for ripping people off. And look, sweetness . . . . you're cute as hell, but I'm not going to keep pushing. No means no. I get it. So give me twenty now and twenty upon delivery. Just tell me where to bring it."

Darla thought about it for a moment, but she knew right away what she was going to end up doing. She handed him over a twenty-dollar bill. He reached through his own window and took it. He seemed to make an extra effort to make sure their hands touched during the exchange.

"Now where should I bring it?"

Darla told him and then rolled her window up right away. He gave her a glowering little smile as he tucked her money into his pocket, and then they parted ways.

As Darla drove out of the parking lot to cruise around her old hometown for a while, she shuddered at the eerie little chill that crept up her spine.

Chapter Twenty Two

When Kate arrived at the station, the disappointed look on Officer Smith's face told her all she needed to know. Apparently, his search for the names of high school dropouts from over the last ten years hadn't panned out. However, when he met her at the front of the lobby, he had a single sheet of paper in his hand. When he handed it over to her, he looked like a sad child, wishing he could have done more to impress his parents.

"What's this?" Kate asked.

"Well, it was harder than I thought to find any a way to come up with the names of people that had dropped out. So I don't have an official list. What I *was* able to do, though, was provide two names I knew for sure had dropped out. I asked Frances, over on dispatch, if she could think of anyone, and she gave me one more name. Sadly, we won't be able to get anything definite until morning when we can call the records office at the school.

"In the meantime, this paper," he said, indicating the sheet he had just handed Kate, "is the result of a study that was done three years ago. Some big-wig from a college in Tennessee came through, saying they were doing a study on high school dropout rates in the southern states. Stateside High School participated in it, and those are the results."

Kate looked the paper over. It was very brief and mostly comprised of numbers. It gave her a snapshot of what she needed, just without any names. The year prior to the study, there were eight hundred and eleven students in Stateside High School. At the end of the year, there were eight hundred and two. A note had been added to the figures, stating that any students that had moved or been relocated were not included in the final count, making a total of five students that had dropped out.

There were similar results in the year the study was conducted. That year, there were six students that dropped out. In the space of two years, there were only eleven students that had willingly stopped attending high school. According to numbers and percentages at the bottom of the page, this was about average with most other schools in the state. Kate figured that meant if she looked back over the course of ten years, she would have about twenty people to look into.

The frustrating aspect of this was that they would not be able to get names. And even when the school hours were underway, tomorrow would be the first day of Thanksgiving break, according to Principal Robinson.

"I've jotted down the three names Frances and I were able to come up with," Smith said. "But one of the names I provided... well, I can promise you they aren't your killer. He moved up to New York. He was posting on Facebook yesterday, so I know he wasn't around here."

Just like that, Kate felt her promising theory start to slip away. Still, though, there was the fact that she now knew what she thought might be used as a murder weapon.

"Any luck on that graduation cap?" Kate asked.

"Not yet. However, I called a man I sometimes play poker with. His oldest daughter graduated two years ago and his wife is a pack rat. He's on the way right now, bringing the entire graduation ensemble."

"Nice work, Smith. Thanks. Sorry to have you calling friends so late."

"He didn't seem to mind. People are getting scared now. I think you'll find that when a small community feels like they're under attack, people start to come together pretty quickly."

Kate knew this, as she had seen it multiple times in the course of her career. But she also knew that such a mentality could often work to the killer's advantage. In a small town, if the killer was local, it was that much easier to keep tabs on the investigation *and* any future victims.

Something about his idea triggered another thought. The killer knew the women were drinking and, in the cases of Kayla and Vanessa, seemed to even know when they would be arriving home. So if he *was* following them, what situations or environments would he be around them in? She wondered if he had been present at the bowling alley when Mariah was killed—not as just some creepy stalker hidden in the shadows, but as an active member of a group.

She felt like there might be something there, but she wasn't quite sure what it was yet.

It was inching closer to 10:30, but Kate knew she would not be able to get back to sleep until she settled her brain down. Even if it was going over criminal background checks of the three names Smith and Frances had given her, she had to do *something*.

She did just that, using the database to start checking the three names she had been given. She had pulled up results from the first one—a man who now owned his own lumber business in Glensville—when Smith knocked on the door to her little office space.

"Got something for you," he said. He showed her a graduation cap, still wrapped nicely in the plastic package it had originally come in.

He tossed it to Kate and she caught it easily. She carefully unwrapped the cap, wanting to respect the owners. When she had it free of its wrapping, she held it up and watched the tassels fall and bounce in the air, attacked by a thin black nylon rope. She set the cap on the table and stretched the tassels out, taking all of the slack out of their decorative frayed ends and the rope that held them to the cap. She guessed it to be right at a foot in length—maybe fourteen inches. It may not wrap completely around a woman's neck, but it would be more than enough to choke her.

Kate ran her fingers along the tassels, thinking. She then took the crime scene photos from Kayla Peterson's death out of her file, as they showed the clearest strangulation marks. Kate leaned in and squinted at the marks and saw some irritation around the bruises, almost like a rubbed sort of mark.

The size and shape of the abrasion was almost a perfect match for the tassels.

With her heart hammering, she picked up her phone again. She tried DeMarco one more time, her excitement overruling the worry that her partner had not answered before. The phone started ringing as Kate continued to look at those tassels which, she had to admit, looked a lot less pretty and celebratory when she pictured them wrapped around a woman's neck.

⚜ ⚜ ⚜

DeMarco was feeling extremely guilty when she and Kate returned to the hotel. In all the time she had known Kate, she could not remember a time where she had ever been this frustrated with her. She knew Kate had not let the little glimpse of fame from being the Miracle Mom go to her head, but she found herself questioning her partner's commitment to her job.

She had never doubted Kate's instincts. The woman had the sort of intuition that could nearly be called supernatural at times. But something was off with Kate now and whatever it might be, it was frustrating the hell out of DeMarco. There was no denying it, but she did not feel like going deep into the issue with Kate.

Instead, almost as soon as DeMarco stepped into her motel room, she turned right back around and stepped back out. She wasn't sure if it was the stress or all of the talk about alcohol, but she found herself in need of a drink. Of course, without a partner to have a drink with, that meant drinking alone in an establishment like Esther's Place, and DeMarco was not quite that desperate.

She knew there was a Quick Stop about a quarter of a mile away from the motel. She knew she couldn't knock a six-pack off by herself, but she'd leave the remnants in her fridge for whoever had the room next. She walked to the car and paused. She was wired with anxious energy and the store was only a quarter of a mile away. She felt a little foolish for making the decision, but she decided to walk. Hell, it might even give her an opportunity to see what the roads looked like after hours—a glimpse into the non-existent night life their killer would be experiencing as he went out to end lives.

DeMarco pulled her collar up, buttoned her jacket, and walked. It was cold, but the chill was almost pleasant. It made her think of Thanksgiving and what it would look like this year. She was single again, which would please her parents, neither of whom had exactly warmed to the fact that she was gay. They were supportive of her sexuality up until she started dating and then that changed everything. Yes, it would suck to be single around the holidays, but a drama-free Thanksgiving with her parents did not seem so bad.

Of course, she and Kate would have to wrap this case in the next day or two in order for either of them to enjoy anything resembling a normal Thanksgiving. She thought of what the holiday might be like for Kate this year—a new baby to go along with her still relatively new grandkid. It really was sort of funny, looking at it as an outsider.

Her thoughts were still on Kate when she arrived at the Quick Stop. Maybe she was being too judgmental. If Kate was going through something, shouldn't DeMarco, as her partner, do her best to support her?

No way I'm finishing a six-pack tonight, she reminded herself. *Might as well have some help.*

She reached into her pocket for her phone and found it wasn't there. She mentally slapped herself when she recalled setting it on the edge of the bed at the motel and not picking it back up. Rolling her eyes at herself, she entered the store. The clerk was wiping down the counters and sliding all of the impulse buy items up. He gave her a curt nod as she walked to the back, where she saw the beer was located. He looked impatient, making DeMarco assume that the place closed at ten o'clock—just seven minutes away according to her watch.

DeMarco picked up a six-pack of Fat Tire and, sympathizing with the clearly bored employee, hurried to the counter. The guy scanned the beer and as she was reaching into her inner coat pocket for her small billfold, the clerk said something she had not been expecting.

"ID?"

"What?" she asked, not sure she'd heard him correctly.

"Sorry, but I need to see ID."

"Oh," she said, chuckling. She plucked her driver's license from the billfold and showed it to him. "I'm actually sort of flattered."

"Yeah, sorry," the kid said, taking her credit card and swiping it in the little machine behind the counter. "Effective three months ago, the state of North Carolina now asks us to card every single person that buys alcohol, regardless of how old they look."

She frowned as she took the bag he pushed her way—a handled plastic one, carrying her beer. "I am officially no longer flattered," she said.

And as the comment left her mouth, an idea occurred to her. A theory, or maybe even a link. She couldn't quite grasp it just yet, but it was there, forming and bubbling to the surface. She needed to talk to Kate before it escaped her entirely.

DeMarco hurried out of the convenience store, bagged beer in hand. When she reached the parking lot, she cursed herself for deciding to walk. She broke into a sprint right away and in her hurry, just barely caught a glimpse of the car parked at the edge of the lot. A girl sat inside, smoking a cigarette and blowing smoke out into the night. DeMarco barely regarded her at all; they were nothing more than strangers passing by one another in the night.

Chapter Twenty Three

Kate had eliminated the three names Smith and Frances had given to her. Still, she studied the report Smith had given her, wondering if there was something there. Really, though, it was only secondary. DeMarco had called four minutes ago, confused as to why she was not in her in her motel room.

"I could ask you the same question," Kate said. She was only half-joking.

"You hung up on the case?" DeMarco asked.

"Yeah. I thought I had a breakthrough, but it's already losing steam. I do think I know what the murder weapon was, though."

"Hang on to that thought. I'll be there in ten minutes."

She actually made in eight. When she came through the door into their little workspace, she looked like a woman possessed. She had something on her mind, something pushing her, and it made her eyes look wild and alive. Her eyes fell on the graduation cap still sitting on the table in front of Kate and a wide smile lit up her face.

"Son of a bitch," DeMarco said. "How'd you figure it out?"

"My curtains told me," Kate said with a grin.

"Sure. Makes sense to me. Holy crap, Kate. I would have never even imagined…"

"So tell me what you've got. Because my latest theory has essentially crashed and burned."

"I've got a six-pack of beer wedged in my mini-fridge back at the hotel that I got carded for. It made me feel great to be carded. But then the cashier told me that it was mandatory. There was a law passed a few months ago that tells all cashiers to card anyone buying alcohol no matter how old they are."

"Okay…"

"So if the killer wants to know the addresses of these girls, he may not have to do much following at all. He might be getting their addresses from their

IDs. And there are lots of IDs being flashed around at bars and convenience stores—especially by girls that have just turned twenty-one."

"Maybe," Kate said. "The only thing, though, is that these girls were underage. So it doesn't quite pan out."

"Exactly. It's going to be pretty easy to spot an underage girl, especially if they're showing their ID in the hopes of getting served or being able to buy a six-pack or a bottle of Boones Farm. And if he's for some reason killing these girls based on them drinking or trying to get away with drinking underage, it would make sense that the killer frequents bars, right. Right there, in that one moment of showing their ID, he's discovering that they aren't of age *and* he's learning where they live. The same could be true of convenience stores, but I think it might be harder."

It was a compelling theory, but not one that Kate thought was logical. The great thing about it, though, was that it would be easy to contact the potential suspects. To her knowledge, there was only one bar in town—two if you counted the little bar area in the bowling alley.

"The only potential problem I see," Kate said, "is that these were all college girls, home from break. There's no guarantee that the killer would have seen the IDs at Esther's, or the bowling alley. It could be some creeper from Charlotte or some other place. Hell, Kayla Peterson went to college in Florida. There's a lot of bars and convenience stores between here and Florida."

"That's correct," DeMarco agreed. "However, I think *your* discovery proves that our guy is a local."

With that said, they looked down at the table. The tassels on the graduation cap seemed to tease them.

"So we need to find where these three girls went on the nights they were killed," Kate said. "We need to see if any of them attempted to buy a drink or showed their IDs for any reason."

"We need to talk to more friends."

Kate instantly thought of Kayla Peterson's friends; she thought particularly of Oliva Macintyre and how she had seemed to be putting on a front. She even remembered pointing out to DeMarco how she thought Olivia might have bene more forthcoming if they'd spoken to her away from her little circle of friends.

"Did you happen to get Olivia Macintyre's phone number?"

DeMarco gave a playful thumbs-up and retrieved her phone from her pocket. She did some scrolling and then placed a call. Kate realized it was nearing eleven o'clock on a Monday night and it might be considered rude to call people at such an hour, but she was willing to piss some people off if it meant getting them closer to finding their killer. He'd already taken three in under a week; there was no telling when he might decide to strike again.

DeMarco made quick work of the call. When she ended it, she still had that excited and wild look in her eyes. "Olivia just happens to be out and about tonight. Visiting with friends. I asked if she could talk without her friends and she said she could. But she asked if we could meet somewhere neutral. Not Esther's Place or the police station. I recommended the hotel and she said that works for her. She's headed there right now."

"That was quick. It didn't take any threats on your end?"

"No. If anything, she sounded nervous. Almost scared."

Kate took a moment to rewrap the graduation cap before she and DeMarco headed back out toward the lobby. She checked her watch as they approached the car and saw that it was 10:50. It wasn't the first time since the sun had gone down that Kate got the impression that this might turn out to be a very long night.

⚜ ⚜ ⚜

Kate was looking out of her room's window and saw the moment that Olivia Macintyre pulled into the lot. She sat in her car for a while, perhaps trying to talk herself out of having a late-night meeting with two FBI agents. When she did finally get out, she walked quickly across the lot. She kept her head tucked down as she speed-walked to the room DeMarco had told her to meet them in. It was quite apparent that Olivia wanted no one to know she was there.

Kate opened the door for her before the girl had time to knock. "Come on in," she said.

DeMarco was sitting on the edge of the bed and gave Olivia a sympathetic stare. "There's no need to be frightened," she said. "Honestly, we just wanted to ask you some follow-up questions."

"That's right," Kate said. "No offense, but it did seem like you were holding back a bit when you were around your friends."

"Maybe a little," Olivia admitted. "You were sort of putting us on the spot, you know?"

"We need to know everywhere you and Kayla went on the night she died," DeMarco said, ignoring the accusation. "You were the only one that spent any time alone with her. So if she said anything to you that might have made you think she was in some sort of trouble, we need to know about it."

"Trust me. I've thought back on that hour or so, wondering if I somehow missed some big clue. But I swear to God, I can't think of anything. She seemed to be in a genuinely great mood."

"Now's the time to level with us, Olivia," Kate said. "Is there anywhere else you and Kayla, or you and any of the other girls, went that night?"

"We were telling the truth. We mostly just stayed at Claire's house."

"Mostly?"

Olivia frowned and shook her head. "Shit. Look . . . I'm sorry, but . . ."

"What is it?"

Kate wasn't sure if it was guilt or fear she was reading on the girl's face. Whichever it was, it was clear she was hiding something. "We went to Esther's Place," she finally said. "We figured since we were in college and the rules have always been sort of loose there anyway, they'd serve us drinks."

"And why did you keep that from us?" Kate asked. She was angry as hell but did her best not to let it show.

"I'm sorry! But it didn't seem wise to admit to FBI agents that we tried to get served underage at a local bar."

"Did they serve you?" DeMarco asked.

"No. It was sort of embarrassing."

"When you tried ordering a drink, did the bartender ask to see your ID?"

"Yeah. Kayla and I gave him ours, just hoping, you know? Half the time, they don't even look at it. You guys know how it is—wear a shirt cut low enough, look at the bartender a certain way, and it's not too difficult. But Claire and Tabby didn't even try. Especially not after me and Kayla got turned down."

"So what happened after that?" Kate asked.

"Nothing. They kicked us out."

"Was there a scene?" Kate asked. "Was it a simple request and then you left, or did it get heated?"

"It got a little heated, yeah. But he was subtle about it. Looking back on it, I guess I'd even say he was professional. He made sure he walked us to the door, sort of corralling us, you know. He opened the door for us, pointed to the parking lot, and told us to get lost. *Get lost.* Those were his exact words.. I wasn't expecting it, really. It's not like we're the first girls to ever try getting served underage."

"Does it work around here sometimes?"

"A few times, I think people have gotten away with it at Esther's Place. But Pauly's is pretty much known for it."

"Pauly's?"

"Yeah, it's this little shit-kicking hole in the wall place right on the edge of town. No one under thirty goes there anymore. It's a dive. Sketchy, boring, and gross. That sort of place. You feel sticky and dirty by just walking in there."

"How have we not heard of this place yet?" Kate wondered out loud.

"We did, but not by name," DeMarco said. "Gates said there were two bars in town, right? The first day we met him."

"Pauly's is hardly a bar, really," Olivia said. "No one under thirty would be caught dead in there."

"Why not?"

"Because it sucks," Olivia said. "Seriously, no one ever goes there. There are like three beers on tap and usually filled with grown men that are just looking for something to do to waste the time before they have to go home to their wives and kids. It's a place for old people to go get drunk and complain about how lazy the youth are and how the country is going to hell. I guarantee you there's nothing on the jukebox newer than 1990."

"You ever been there?"

"Kayla and I tried it one time last summer because we were pretty sure they'd serve us. But one look at the place and we bounced. It's skeezy."

"The night she died, when you went to Esther's Place, do you know if the bartender called the police on you?"

"I don't think so. He said he would if we didn't leave right away. But we all left right after that. Like I said, we weren't expecting the bartender to get that upset with us. So after that, we stopped pushing our luck. That's when we ended up going to Claire's house."

"Did this guy get rough with you?"

"No. He escorted us to the door and got sort of loud. I do remember he was looking at Kayla sort of... I don't know. Not creepy, but just not pleasant. Like he might have been trying to imagine what she'd look like naked. Then again, Kayla got that look from a lot of guys."

"She ever mention any guys from college that might have been causing her problems?"

"No. She mentioned this one guy she hooked up with a few times, but it was all good. Nothing bad or dangerous or anything like that."

Kate and DeMarco shared a brief look which was broken when DeMarco asked: "How long is Esther's open on weeknights?"

"Until midnight, I think."

Kate checked her watch and saw that it was 11:25. "Then I think we need to get going."

DeMarco nodded and stood from her place on the edge of the bed. "Olivia, thank you for meeting with us. I think that's all we need for now."

Olivia walked to the door, looking a little ashamed. "Did I screw things up by not telling you guys about the bar in the first place?" she asked. "Like, did it hinder the investigation?"

"Maybe not," Kate said. "It's too early to tell."

Olivia nodded and opened the door. When she left the room, Kate and DeMarco followed behind her. Olivia had said Esther's Place closed at midnight, which gave them about thirty-five minutes to get there and speak to someone before they closed for the night. They got into their car as Olivia pulled away, following her back out into a night-shrouded Harper Hills.

Chapter Twenty Four

Kate felt like they were currently working with a lot of different dots, but no real thread to connect them all. She was very aware of this as they entered Esther's Place yet again. The Monday night crowd was small; only two tables were occupied, and four seats were taken at the bar. The bartender on duty was a middle-aged female. She was currently speaking to one of the men at the bar, leaning forward and speaking as he glared at the television behind the bar.

She turned her attention to the agents as they approached the bar. Something about sidling up to the bar at 11:30 at night made Kate feel incredibly tired. She snickered a bit internally when she tried to think of the last time she'd been in a bar at such an hour.

The bartender excused herself from her current conversation and came over to the other end of the bar where Kate and DeMarco were sitting. "You ladies are becoming regulars," she joked. She then extended her hand and said, "We've not been properly introduced. My name is Vicki Sellers."

Kate and DeMarco took turns shaking her hand. As they did, Kate did her best to size the woman up. She was likely around forty or forty-five. She was nice-looking but not the sort of attractive woman you usually wanted working a bar during the later hours. She looked a little tired herself but also carried a sort of quiet resolve that Kate assumed most female bartenders needed to possess.

"Could we talk to you for a moment?" Kate asked.

"Sure," Vicki said. "As you can see, we're not exactly pumping right now."

"How often would you say you have to kick out underage kids that are trying to get served?"

A sudden understanding sank into Vicki's eyes and she sighed deeply. "Not too often, though I'm guessing you got wind of the incident I had on Wednesday night."

"We did," DeMarco said. "Would you mind giving us your version of it?"

"Well, I wasn't the one that was tending bar," Vicki said. "It was actually a pretty slow night for the bar, so I was over in the kitchen area, helping them wrap up for the night. But as I was coming out, I saw one of our other bartenders, Brent, escorting these two girls towards the door. The girls looked a little upset, but Brent was calm and polite—just like we ask our bartenders to be when something like that comes up."

"Did Brent tell you what happened?" Kate asked.

"Yes, he filled me in right away. Just two girls trying to get served underage. There were two other girls with them. They all left together. Of course, as you probably already know, one of them was Kayla Peterson. Brent felt awful the next day when he found out she had been killed. He sort of railed on them, you know?"

Both Kate and DeMarco nodded in sympathy. Kate was pretty sure DeMarco was thinking the same thing as she was: *Fake sorrow over something like that would be a great cover for sure.*

"Do you know which of the girls showed their IDs?" Kate asked.

"I know for sure Kayla did because Brent told me about it the following day. As for the other girls, I don't know for sure."

"Any chance Brent is here tonight?"

"Sorry, no. But you might catch him over at Pauly's. Brent is sort of a freelancer." She chuckled at this for a moment and added: "It's a small town with only three places to get a drink. And Brent is pretty good at what he does. He sort of subs in and out at all three, though I don't think he's worked the bowling alley in a while."

"So you're saying he comes and goes, working at whatever bar might need him?"

"Yeah. Sometimes when it's a busy weekend like the Fourth of July or Labor Day, he likes to haggle. He knows about a hundred drink recipes and isn't too bad too look at, so the single ladies tend to buy more. On those weekends, he sometimes goes with the highest bidder."

"Any idea when Pauly's closes?" Kate asked.

Vicki sneered as she gave her answer. "Who knows. There are no real hours to speak of. They don't open until five in the afternoon. Some nights they'll close at ten or eleven, some nights not until two in the morning. Depends on who's tending bar and how many are there."

"We heard from someone in the younger crowds in town that it's sort of a shithole," DeMarco said.

"I could see how a younger person might think so. Pauly's caters more to working people and, if I'm being honest and a little mean, where all of the ... *seasoned* drinkers go. It's where older folks go to bitch about politics and tear up a dartboard."

"How often does Brent work there?" Kate asked.

"Maybe two nights a week. I know he's there tonight and will probably be there until they close."

"Thank you," Kate said.

The agents gave a nod of appreciation as they got up and headed for the door. On their way across the parking lot, Kate caught something out of the corner of her eye—a familiar face she nearly overlooked in her hurry to get back to the car. She stopped and turned to her left just to make sure.

"Hey, DeMarco?"

DeMarco turned to look as well. Both agents took a moment to realize that Jenna Marshall was parked at the far end of the parking lot. She had obviously parked there to remain unseen, but had poorly judged the angle of the farthest streetlight. It was essentially highlighting the passenger side of her car, clearly showing her face.

Kate started walking in that direction. It took DeMarco a while to understand what Kate was up to, so she fell in a few steps behind. As they approached Jenna's car, the young woman noticed them. Her eyes grew wide, so when she rolled them, it was very apparent. It was also apparent when she said, "Oh shit," though neither Kate nor DeMarco could actually hear her.

Kate motioned for Jenna to roll the window down, which the girl did right away. Before Kate could say a single word, Jenna was pleading her case.

"I know, you heard my folks bitch about being here," she said. "You aren't going to tell them, are you?"

"That's your own business to deal with," Kate said, approaching the car and leaning slightly inside the opened window. "Although that changes if you're back here looking to buy more drugs."

"So," DeMarco said, falling in beside Kate. "Why *are* you here, Jenna?"

"I don't even know. I came out tonight just to ride around and listen to music... sort of travel down some of the back roads I used to take when I was in high school. But I ended up back here. Just sitting, seeing who would show up."

"You *sure* we won't see someone pull in soon, thinking you're here to buy more mushrooms or something else?"

"I swear."

"We'll take your word for it for now," Kate said.

"Jenna, it's sort of fate that you're here right now," DeMarco said. "We need to ask you some questions about the night Vanessa died. Can you handle that?"

"I'm not sure what else you need to know. I told you everything."

"Maybe, and maybe not."

"Jenna," Kate said, "did you and Vanessa try getting drinks anywhere in town that night?"

Jenna frowned, looking down to her feet by the gas and brake pedals. This pretty much gave the agents their answer.

"You aren't in trouble for it," Kate said. "We're just trying to form some links."

"Yes. Yes, we did. It was stupid but we were feeling… I don't know. We were feeling adventurous, I guess. Vanessa was having problems, coming back from school and being reminded of this stupid town. She wanted to act out. So we got some drinks. It wasn't until the third round that the guy asked for our ID."

"Here, at Esther's Place?"

"No way. They're super tight about that sort of thing. We went to Pauly's. Two pretty girls on a Sunday night, the bartender didn't even think twice about it. Not at first, anyway."

"What happened when he asked for ID?"

"Ah man, he was pissed. Like, gritting his teeth and fuming. So I paid him in cash for what we'd already drank and we got out of there. It was sort of unsettling, so I called up my friend that sold us the mushrooms."

"Would you happen to know this bartender's name?" DeMarco asked.

"Brent Clarkson. He's pretty well known because he's sort of a hottie."

And that was what they had been looking for. One man, one link between at least two of the victims. Mariah Ogden would be a bit harder to pin down because she had been killed at the bowling alley. But then Kate recalled that

Vicki, the bartender at Esther's tonight, had told them that Brent did tend bar at the bowling alley every now and then.

"That's all for now, Jenna," DeMarco said. "Now please go home. I hate to sound motherly and all, but—"

"I'll sound motherly, then," Kate said. "Go home, Jenna. It's getting dangerous out here and there's nothing in this parking lot or in that bar that's going to keep you safe."

Jenna gave a small nod and rolled her window back up. Kate was pleased to see that Jenna was pulling out of the parking lot before she and DeMarco had made it back to their car.

Chapter Twenty Five

Finding directions to Pauly's was as simple as plugging the name and the town into the maps app on Kate's phone. The ride from Esther's Place to Pauly's only took eleven minutes. Before they arrived, Kate couldn't help but wonder if they had somehow gotten lost. The veering back roads had nearly made her decide to call ahead to see if Brent was even working there tonight. But there was no sense in clueing him in. Making such a call in a small town might be dangerous. If Brent answered the phone, he could easily leave before they arrived; if anyone else answered the phone and considered Brent a friend, they could easily warn him.

So she decided not to make the call. She started to regret that decision as the directions took them down a winding back road that, according to the map, would take them out of town and to a route that was nothing but back roads for another twenty miles.

"Shit, passed it," DeMarco said suddenly.

Kate looked out the window on DeMarco's side as she came to a stop and put the car into reverse. Being past midnight on a thin back road, there was no traffic coming from behind to prevent this. After about fifty feet, a small place did indeed come into view on the left. The place itself stood out fairly well; the fact that it was about twenty yards off the road and surrounded by nothing more than forest on all sides made it hard to locate unless you knew it was there.

Pauly's was a simple little one-story building. If Kate had passed it during the day on her way to somewhere else, she would have assumed it was just an old abandoned store of some kind, ignored and dried up since going out of business many years ago. But at night, there was a notable glow coming from the windows. There were also four vehicles parked in the little haphazard gravel lot in front of the place, three trucks and one beat-up old sedan. An old corrugated sign hung over the front door, reading, in faded red letters illuminated by two simple lights above, PAULY'S.

DeMarco pulled the car in slowly. Maybe it was because of the isolated location, but the place had an ominous vibe to it. Even without stepping foot inside, Kate could understand why the younger crowd would have nothing to do with the place.

When they did step inside, Kate found herself in the doorway of a place that looked like the carbon copy of every small bar in a rural town out of movies from the seventies and eighties. There were no bells and whistles, no frills or cultural allure. There was an old battered jukebox against the far wall, currently playing something by Randy Travis, and two well-worn dartboards beside that. Two men were currently playing a game on one of them.

The bar was a crude-looking length of wood that took up almost the entire right wall, leaving a floor space of only twenty feet or so. There were five tables, several chairs, and two booths in that cramped space. There were three men sitting at the bar, hunched over glasses of beer. There was no TV behind the bar, just several shelves with liquor and an antique-looking glass out of some other long ago bar.

Including the bartender, there were six people in Pauly's. All six of them turned to look at the two women who appeared to randomly visit this hole in the wall bar just after midnight. One of the men at the bar was making no effort to hide the fact that he was checking DeMarco out. He, like the other two men at the bar, looked worn out, tired, and as if they had spent a great percentage of their adult lives sitting at a bar.

The place reeked of desperation. It felt like the sort of place people came to after they had given up on their lives—the sort of place where a lot of paychecks had likely been drained before Friday night had even come to a close.

"Can I help you ladies?" the bartender asked. Kate figured this was Brent Clarkson. Vicki from Esther's Place had told them he'd be here, after all. But Kate found herself rather confused. Jenna Marshall had described Brent Clarkson as a hottie. The man they were currently looking at was, Kate hated to think, not good-looking at all. He was fifty or so, going bald up top with the rest of his hair in disarray. He tried smiling at them and it was not the sort of smile that would have girls quivering. Kate thought it was a smile that might make younger children afraid, actually.

"Can we see you at the end of the bar?" DeMarco asked.

He gave them a perplexed look but did as they asked. One of the men at the bar chuckled at this.

"What is it?" he asked as he neared the end of the bar.

"Are you Brent Clarkson?" DeMarco asked quietly.

"No."

"Is he here?"

"No." Apparently, this bartender was not much of a talker.

"Do you know where he might be?" Kate asked.

"Probably home by now, I'd say."

"So he does fill in here from time to time?"

"That's right. He was here earlier, but things got slow. We flipped a coin to see who could go home first."

"Do you know Mr. Clarkson well?"

"Well enough. Now… who are you, exactly?"

Kate slowly and subtly slid her badge and ID up on the bar. The bartender eyed it closely and then looked up to them with bewildered eyes. He took a shaky step away from the bar as if he thought they might be there for him.

"Do you serve underage kids here?" DeMarco asked.

"Never knowingly."

"But from what I understand, there's a new law. You have to card no matter how old the person looks, right?"

"Oh yeah. But Brent thinks every woman that walks in here wants to bang him. Sad thing is, a lot of them do. So sometimes he lets it slide. But only here. He couldn't really get away with it at Esther's Place."

"We understand he might have served someone here last night that was underage."

"That he did," the man said. "Although, according to him, he honestly didn't know she was underage. And as far as him not carding… he seems to conveniently forget it when there's a pretty girl involved."

"And he was working here tonight, you say?" Kate asked.

"He was. Had about ten people in earlier. That's a pretty busy night for us on a Monday. I guess it's because Thanksgiving is coming up and a lot of people sort of kick off of work early in the week."

"Was there anyone young in here tonight?" Kate asked.

"I'm not too sure," he said. "When Brent was here, I was over there playing darts for a while. Had to drive two drunk assholes home, too."

"Any idea if Brent had any run-ins with underage drinkers tonight?"

"If he did, I didn't see it."

One of the men at the bar laughed at this. It was a mocking sort of laugh, as if he were making fun of something.

"Something funny?" DeMarco asked with ice in her tone.

"Nope," the man said. "Not funny. But Brent did have himself a little run-in tonight. Pretty little thing came in tonight around nine or so—just after he drove the drunkies home," he said, nodding to the bartender.

"What happened?" Kate asked. She was barely aware that her legs were already starting to carry her toward the door. Every nerve in her body sensed that this could be it—the information that helped them close this case and find their killer.

"The girl came up to the bar like she'd been doing it forever and ordered a drink from Brent. He started making it—some fruity thing with vodka, I think—and asked her for her ID as he was making it. She said something to him in a soft voice, flirting with him. But she slid that ID over to him. He checked it out and when he saw it, you would have thought she had reached across the bar and slapped him in the face. He pushed it right back, dumped her drink right in front of her, and told her to get out. Actually, he told her to 'get the hell out before I call the police and your parents.' She called him a few names and then busted ass out of here."

"Was that it?" Kate asked.

"Yeah, Brent didn't really say much of anything. But man did he look pissed off. He was the sort of mad that makes you think either someone's head is going to explode or a fight is about to start, you know?"

"How long ago was that?" DeMarco asked. "You said nine or so?"

The man shrugged. "Couldn't have been any later than nine thirty when she left. Maybe nine forty-five at the latest."

DeMarco directed her attention back to the bartender. "How long ago did Brent Clarkson leave here?"

"Maybe half an hour."

"And he said he was going home?"

"Not trying to be difficult, but he didn't say. And I didn't ask."

"Well, what about the girl?" Kate asked. A sudden sense of urgency started to flood her. From an overhead view, the entire ordeal probably didn't look like much. But her heart was thrumming and there was a stirring in her pulse. She knew they were on to something.

"What about her?" the bartender said.

"Did either of you know her?" DeMarco asked. There was urgency in her tone. She was picking up on the tension, too.

"Hell, I don't know," the bartender said. "I barely remember seeing her."

"Pretty sure her last name is Dowdy," the guy at the bar said. "Her dad used to be a foreman out at the sawmill on the edge of town before it shut down. His name is Kenny Dowdy. She looks just like her dad. Don't know her name, though."

"How old do you think she was?"

"After she was gone, Brent said she was just twenty," the man said. "Her driver's license showed that she was about six months shy of twenty-one."

"Any idea where the Dowdys live?"

The man and the bartender exchanged a look and Kate saw that they felt it, too. Something was going on—something bad, maybe. They felt that they were being involved in something pivotal. The man at the bar was clearly buzzed and likely on his way to being blitzed, but in that moment, his eyes looked clear and a little worried.

"Out on Crabtree Road," the guy at the bar said. "I don't know the address, but it's the fourth or fifth house down the road, on the right. Can't see it from the road, but you can see the driveway pretty clearly. There's this decorative fence made with old cross-ties."

"Thank you," Kate said, already pushing herself away from the bar.

Sensing that he was actually helping, the man continued assisting even as Kate and DeMarco opened the door and headed outside.

"Take a right outta here, then another right onto Springer Road a few miles down. It crosses over onto Crabtree after about five or six miles."

Kate latched on to the information because that was one other thing she had learned in her time with the bureau: that the rambling directions of a local could beat the sometimes fickle accuracy of a GPS any day.

Chapter Twenty Six

The almost-drunk man's directions seemed to be on point. DeMarco had turned onto Springer Road a few moments ago and was now doing eighty-five down a straight yet narrow two-lane. It was scary to see the night-traced road go blazing by but Kate could not deny the surge of adrenaline that pushed through her as she pressed back into her seat.

It then occurred to her that this could be a double-play sort of situation. Doing anything she could to take her mind off of DeMarco's speed, Kate took out her phone and called up the Harper Hills PD. She was surprised when Gates answered the phone rather than Smith.

"Sheriff Gates, what are you doing in so late? Or early . . ."

"Got a call from Officer Smith that it seemed like you ladies might be on to something. Want to tell me what this graduation cap I'm looking at led you to?"

"I'll be happy to in the morning. Right now, I need you to do something for me. I need you to get the address for Brent Clarkson and send a unit over to his apartment."

Gates chuckled. "That unit would be me and Smith. Actually, maybe just me, while Smith stays here and mans the station."

"That's fine. Could you please go check the place out and just make sure he's there? If he is, do you mind just parking somewhere nearby and keeping an eye out?"

"I can do that," Gates said. "Do I need to treat him as a suspect?"

"Yes. Take any measures necessary and assume he's a prime suspect."

"I'm on it. I'll contact you with details when I have them."

They ended the call just as DeMarco came to a slight bend in the road. She lowered her speed, though not much. The screeching of tires filled the night for a moment and it did Kate some good to realize that she still enjoyed the thrill of it all.

Crabtree Road came up on the right as Springer merged into it three miles later. "You know," DeMarco said. "In terms of motive, this would be lame. I mean, are we going on the assumption that this guy is killing girls that try to get a drink underage? And if so, we have no hard proof that he was even working at the bowling alley on the night Mariah Ogden was killed."

"That's exactly right," Kate said. "But you feel it, right? You feel that sense of everything falling into place."

"I do," she said. "I've sort of sensed it before, but not this strong. It's him, isn't it? Brent Clarkson is the killer."

"Either that or he knows who is. Or, at the very least, why these girls are being killed."

"That's house number three," DeMarco said, nodding to the side of the road.

And then, just as the bar patron had said, the next driveway that came into view was bordered by a decorative half-fence of cross-ties on both sides. Had they not been looking for it, the fences would have been missed in the darkness of night. The guy at the bar had also been correct in that the Dowdy house was just off of the road, though not far; the moment DeMarco pulled into the driveway, they could see the shape of the house at the bottom of a little hill. The gravel driveway that led to it was nicely maintained and ended in a small circle.

There were two vehicles parked in the driveway. One was a newer model car and the other was an older truck. The truck was still on, the taillights glowing cherry red in the dark.

As DeMarco pulled further down the driveway, Kate got a decent view of the front of the house. It was a modest little home, probably what would be considered average in Harper Hills. As she took in the house and the yard beyond, she caught movement coming off of the porch steps, and it was moving fast.

"DeMarco, stop the car!"

DeMarco did just that, not asking questions. Before she had even managed to put it into park, Kate had opened her door and was stepping out of it. "Movement on the right side of the house," she said. "Something running."

Kate was around the hood of the car and giving chase by the time DeMarco had gotten out to follow behind her.

"FBI, stop right there!" Kate cried. Her hand was hovering over her gun, but she had not drawn it yet.

She could just barely see the shadowed figure. It was making a run for the trees. If the figure made it to the tree line, it may be an incredibly short chase—especially if it was someone who knew the town well.

"I said *stop!*" she bellowed.

When the figure still did not stop, Kate drew her weapon and pushed ahead harder, running through the darkened yard. She couldn't see every well, as the only light came from behind her, from the headlights of their car. The light stretched her shadow across the side of the yard, mingling with DeMarco's as she quickly caught up.

"Damn," Kate said. "I can't see him and—"

The words were cut off as the air was taken from her lungs. As she dashed forward, whatever muscles she had strained in her right leg while sweeping Howard Schuler seemed to go absolutely rigid. There was a dull flare of pain in that leg, nearly making her pitch forward into the grass on her face. She halted, coming to a sudden stop, biting back a moan of pain.

"Kate?" DeMarco asked. "You okay?"

"Yeah," she said, embarrassed.

DeMarco only hesitated for a moment. She continued running toward the forest, trying to catch up with the figure before he slipped into the trees. Kate heard DeMarco yell at the man to stop one more time, but he was not listening. Kate watched until she could only see the murky shape of DeMarco running to the woods. She knew DeMarco was fast, but the figure had a head start. Kate hated to not be there with her, helping to run the figure—likely the killer—down.

Instead, she hobbled forward few steps, decided her leg was not going to loosen up any time soon, and stood in place. She looked to the right, where an elm tree sat about fifteen feet away from the house. She leaned against it, taking some of the weight off of her leg. As she did, a flicker of light shone behind her. She turned and saw that someone inside had turned the porch light on.

The front door opened slowly and a young woman poked her head out. This, Kate assumed, was the Dowdy girl they were looking for. And simply putting two and two together told Kate that their arrival had scared the killer away moments before he'd made his way to the porch.

But something doesn't quite seem right about that. She was already home and inside. The other victims weren't.

Too many inconsistencies were piling up, making Kate wonder if they were wrong about this lead, too. Looking to the girl on the porch, it was hard to accept that one wrong decision, and she could have potentially been killed.

⚜ ⚜ ⚜

DeMarco heard the figure—presumably Brent Clarkson—enter the forest just ahead of her. She knew if he managed to get into the thickness of the trees and knew the lay of the land at all, she'd lose him. She holstered her gun and put all of her focus on running. She sprinted harder than she had in quite some time, only slowing the slightest bit when she crossed over into the woods.

She saw several unopened beer cans scattered on the ground. A few seconds later, she saw the empty cardboard container they had been in. She assumed the figure ahead of her had been carrying them, maybe bringing them over for a visit with Darla Dowdy.

She heard his footfall slowing a bit, then speeding up. To keep track of his sounds, she made sure her feet fell softly rather than pounding the ground. It was apparently not a tactic the man ahead of her was accustomed to. The sound of his passage through the woods was very noisy; it sounded like a bear passing through.

It was because of this that she was aware of when he stumbled and tripped. The thundering crash of foliage was only slightly ahead of her and to the right. She unholstered her Glock again and strafed in that direction. She spotted him in the darkened shadows just as he was getting to his feet.

"Freeze right where you are," she said. "I'm an FBI agent, and I *am* armed."

"But I haven't even done anything," he protested.

"Then you had no need to run, now did you?"

"But I—"

"Hands on your head," DeMarco said, stepping in closer. She used her free hand to retrieve her cuffs.

"I swear, I don't know what you think I did!"

"Well, we can figure all of that out somewhere else. For now, I'd really just like to get out of these woods."

She approached him from behind, wrenching his arms down behind his back and slapping on the handcuffs. She then gave him a little push forward, back toward the extremely faint glow of what looked like a porch light that had just come on.

⚜ ⚜ ⚜

"Who's there?" the girl asked on the porch asked. She looked and sounded scared. And, to Kate's frazzled mind, she also looked quite a bit like Kayla Peterson for a moment.

"Agent Kate Wise, FBI." She hobbled away from the tree and stepped closer to the porch. Behind her, she could hear a male voice protesting something, followed by a rustling of leaves and other foliage. "This is the Dowdy residence, right?"

"Yes."

"And what's your name?"

"Darla." The girl came out onto the porch, arms wrapped around herself to ward off the chill of the very early November morning. "What's going on? Why are you here?"

"My partner is giving chase to a man we believe was going to lure you out of your home to harm you."

The girl looked alarmed at first and then looked out to the driveway. She let out a curse and shook her head. "No, no, he's fine. This is all messed up. Shit."

"What?"

"I know him. Sort of. I told him to come over here."

"Are your parents home?"

"No. They went to Raleigh to see some friends of theirs for an early Thanksgiving."

"And you just invited this guy over?"

Darla Dowdy looked out toward the yard, in the direction of where DeMarco and the possible intruder had been running. Kate followed her gaze and saw DeMarco coming out of the tree line. She was pushing a man along. His hands were cuffed behind his back and he stumbled forward as DeMarco gave him a push.

"Who is he, then?" Kate asked, looking back to Darla.

"I don't know his name."

"And you still invited him over?"

"He was bringing me something."

"Drugs?" Kate asked.

"No. Well, not really."

DeMarco was close enough to have heard some of this. As she pushed the cuffed man forward, she nodded back toward the forest. "He was carrying a twelve-pack of beer," she said. "He ditched it when he realized he wasn't going to be able to outrun me."

Kate looked back up to the porch. "That's what he was bringing you?"

"Yes," Darla said, suddenly looking rather frightened. "Am I in trouble or something?"

"No," DeMarco said. "Your friend here, though, I'm not so sure..."

Kate turned to look at the man. He was a little shy of thirty years old from the looks of it. He looked nearly as scared as Darla, looking back and forth between the agents as if he was convinced he was having a dream and was waiting to wake up.

"Do you tend bar around Harper Hills?" she asked.

"What? No. No... I was just bringing her some beer. She paid me the money and—"

"So you weren't working out at Pauly's tonight?"

"No!"

"So what *do* you do?" DeMarco asked. "Besides buying booze for underage girls, that is."

"I work at the ABC store over in Glensville. I do some part-time stuff for a garage on the weekends."

"Why are you in Harper Hills on a Monday night?" Kate asked.

"Just trying to make some extra money."

Kate and DeMarco shared a glance and a shrug. "Well, since you and I are already well-acquainted," DeMarco told him, "we're going to have a little chat. Agent Wise, would you go speak to our new friend on the porch just to make sure it all checks out?"

It made the most sense as far as Kate was concerned. Darla was apparently naïve enough to think that a man like this would be perfectly fine to simply drop off some booze after midnight and not try to push for more. But she also apparently did not know him. So they were either lying, or the guy bringing the beer had the worst luck in the world.

"Come on, Ms. Dowdy," Kate said, walking up the porch steps and doing her best not to cringe at the pain in her right leg. "Let's go have a chat."

Before they went inside, Kate turned back to DeMarco. Yes, she had felt like this case had belonged to DeMarco from the start, but she felt she had to insert her opinions from time to time, especially in a circumstance like this.

"I'm also going to call Gates," she said. "We need an APB out on Brent Clarkson right away. Might even want to consider getting some State PD in as well."

DeMarco nodded, though it was clear that she was disappointed. She apparently did not like the idea of her case being flooded. Kate understood it; she'd felt it herself numerous times in the past. Calling an APB or seeking reinforcements often made overzealous agents feel like failures.

Kate looked away and followed Darla inside, feeling the slightest bit of that disappointment as well.

Chapter Twenty Seven

"I swear, I'd never seen him before in my life. Not until tonight."

Kate pretty much believed her right away. The girl was bewildered to the point of trembling. Even after she and Kate went inside, she held her arms close to her body, hands clutching her elbows as if she were cold. Kate had eyed her to look for any signs of guilt while she had spoken to Gates, suggesting the APB.

"So how did he end up here?"

"Because I asked him to by me beer. He's sort of known for it—this guy that rides around through town looking for teenagers that need someone to buy it for them."

"Any idea how long he's been doing it?"

"At least since my senior year of high school. So that's three years."

"You know his name?"

"No. We just always knew it was the guy in the red truck with a Metallica bumper sticker."

"Never heard any rumors or stories about him at all?"

"Well, sure. Let's be real... no offense. An older guy that is happy to buy underage kids booze. There were all kinds of stories floating around about how he was always willing to take payment other than cash from girls. As far as I know, a few even took hm up on it, but I don't have proof."

"How did the meeting with him go earlier tonight? Did he try to push himself on you?"

"No. I mean there were two times where he suggested that I could pay in other ways, but when I told him no, that was it. One of the reasons I decided to try him out tonight was because I'd been hearing the stories about him for so long. But none of them were bad stories. Other than the rumors girls that were willing, I never heard any bad or crude stories, you know? I figured he was safe."

"But to invite him to your home while your parents were out of town . . . come on, Darla."

"I know," she said. There was anger in her voice, either at herself or at Kate for lecturing her. "It wasn't my smartest decision."

"Well, unless you have anything else to add, I think we're done here."

"No, nothing to add. I invited him, so he wasn't like breaking in or trespassing or anything. But . . . do you have to tell my parents about this?"

"No. But if he is formally arrested, they'll be notified that someone was arrested on their property while they were gone."

Darla nodded, though it didn't look like she was even registering the information. Distracted, she asked: "Does this have something to do with the girls that have been murdered?"

"We can't give details, but we *are* investigating it and as we were looking into bartenders tonight, yes . . . your name came up when we stopped by Pauly's."

Darla nodded again, close to tears. She walked to the door and opened it. "Thanks for . . . I don't know . . . trying to protect me, I guess."

"Of course," Kate said. When she saw the lost desperation in her eyes, it made her think of some of the issues Melissa had gone through when she'd been this young woman's age. It made her homesick in a way she had not felt in a very long time—not only for Melissa, but for Michael and Allen, too.

She stepped back out onto the porch and saw that the cuffed man was sitting on the porch. He was speaking to DeMarco and though she listened closely, it was apparent that she was disappointed.

"One second," DeMarco said, cutting him off. She then nodded to Kate and they walked several feet away from the porch. Kate noticed that Darla Dowdy had closed the door behind her, apparently no longer trusting the man as much as she had earlier in the night.

"Did you get anything useful out of her?" DeMarco asked.

"It's apparently just a huge mix-up," Kate said. She went on to recount everything Darla had told her. "How about you?"

"Well, he's definitely not Brent Clarkson. His name is Kevin Masters. He's fessed up to regularly distributing booze to minors which, as you know, is going to get him *at least* a hefty fine. He says he's aware of the murders in town, though he's only heard about two. He has alibis for two of the three nights a young woman was killed. So, if they check out..."

"Dead end," Kate said, nodding. "So what the hell did we miss?"

"Maybe nothing," DeMarco said. "We still have the *actual* bartender to look for. You get in touch with Gates?"

"I did. He's organizing a team right now, and sending out the all-points bulletin."

As they let the updated information settle in, Kate once again thought of how easily Darla Dowdy could have been killed. If Kevin Masters had been the type to rape or kill, her night could have turned out very different. She wondered what was going on in Darla's life that would have convinced her to make such a foolish decision.

Wow, you are really feeling the mom vibes tonight, aren't you? The voice in her head sounded a lot like Melissa, nearly making her smile in spite of herself.

"Kate, are you okay?"

"Yeah, just zoning out."

DeMarco have Kate a pleading look, but one that was almost politely saying *"Don't bullshit me."*

"What's wrong with the leg?" DeMarco asked.

"I strained something in it when I swept Schuler yesterday."

"Is it okay?"

"Yeah, I think it's just a tweaked muscle or nerve or something."

"Kate, I have to be the bitch on this one. I think you should stay here with the girl just in case Clarkson does come looking for her."

"You're not being a bitch. That's the smart play."

"I know that even if he was coming after her next, our visit probably scared him off and he won't show up. But it's not a chance I want to take. You understand that, right?"

"I do," Kate said with a smile. "DeMarco, it's okay. This is your case and you're clearly the better agent to go out into a chase-type situation right now. So go do your job."

DeMarco gave a nod of appreciation, but there was also something like pride there, too. Both of them understood one pivotal thing in that moment; it was not something that was spoken out loud or even heavily implied, really.

It was the passing of the torch. Kate was happy to pass it on and she could think of no one better to pass it to.

"You call me if he does show up here, though," DeMarco said.

"Absolutely. And I'll send Kevin Masters packing, too."

They both looked back over toward the cuffed man, still sitting on the porch steps. When he saw them looking his way, he looked away quickly as if pretending he hadn't been trying to listen in on their conversation.

But they both knew Clarkson showing up after the FBI had already interrupted the night would be a very slim chance. Kate would essentially be babysitting Darla Dowdy until DeMarco and Gates cleared things up in their search for Brent Clarkson.

There was no need to say anything else. To do so would be overly sentimental, and though they had grown much closer since their first case together, neither of them had ever been a fan of sentiment. Kate walked over to the porch, plucking her little lock-pick kit from her inner pocket. She had always kept her spare handcuff key in this kit, a trick she had picked up from some other agent many years ago. She was slightly saddened that she could not remember the agent or the case.

That's because it's been a long career, she told herself. It was something she was very proud of, that huge chunk of her life that had been spent pursuing justice and saving lives. She felt it all around her as she uncuffed Kevin Masters.

"Go home, Mr. Masters. And I will be telling Sheriff Gates to keep an eye out for you. Please stop doing this."

It occurred to her that Masters might have been the source of the alcohol that had resulted in Jonathan Bowen's tragic accident. She decided not to ask, though. After the scare he'd just had, he'd lie about it, anyway. Besides, what good would it do to out him for it other than make him feel miserable and potentially guilty. She thought the scare she and DeMarco had put into him would suffice.

Kate remained on the porch steps as she watched Kevin Masters get into his truck. He left quickly, kicking up some gravel as he backed out. Kate remained there, watching the taillights disappear in the night. Left alone on the porch, she felt strange. She felt as if there was a door closing behind her, slowly falling into the frame.

She thought of DeMarco, on the hunt for Brent Clarkson. She thought of a man somewhere out there who was killing women with a tassel from an old high school graduation cap.

And she thought about what her life might look like if this did indeed end up being her final case. Would she be okay with that? Would she be able to look back onto this cold night and find it satisfying?

That, she couldn't answer.

But she knew she would have to decide sooner rather than later, and that knowledge made the night feel that much colder, She turned her back to the driveway and headed back inside with Darla Dowdy, leaving the cold and those thoughts for the night to hide.

Chapter Twenty Eight

When the younger agent turned away from her partner and started back for their car, a smile touched the corner of Brent Clarkson's face.

He'd been fully prepared to turn around and call it a night. After all, there had been enough hiccups in his pursuit of killing Darla Dowdy. First, the moron with the beer had showed up just as Brent had started creeping across the yard. Brent had rushed to the woods on the right side of the house, ducking down behind a large copse of trees.

Then, less than a minute later, the other car had come—the car with the FBI agents.

Brent had remained where he was, watching the entire series of events unfold. He realized how incredibly lucky he was that the idiot with the beer had taken off running to the left when the agents showed up. If he'd run to the right, things could have been very bad.

He'd watched as the two agents went running off after the man and then watched them split up. The older agent had taken Darla inside to speak while the younger one had stayed outside with the now-cuffed man. Their voices has carried on the frigid air, but not well enough for Brent to hear much of it. But really, he didn't need to hear any of it. He knew they were here, looking for him and not the moron that had been delivering the beer. He'd known the FBI was in town for a day or so now and had figured he'd end up facing them. He'd just had no idea it would be this quick.

He'd been on the verge of leaving but the agents then made a decision that, in his estimation, was pretty stupid. They were splitting up. Not only that, but the younger and more athletic one was leaving. That meant the older one would be here with Darla. And it was this new bit of information that caused Brent to smile and to stick with his original plan.

In watching the night's events unfold in the Dowdys' front yard, he'd seen this older agent freeze up when they had taken off after the beer delivery guy. She'd pulled a muscle or cramped up or something. Even now, as he watched her walk back toward the porch while her partner left, he could see that she was favoring her left side.

Remaining in the trees, Brent considered his options. He knew that killing an FBI agent would bring some serious heat on him. But Darla would be the fourth victim and he figured that would also bring some heat on him. He knew there was no way this ended without him going to jail—and that was why he was fully prepared to kill himself if he was ever caught.

He hated the idea of suicide. Not because he was afraid of it, but because it's the route his father had taken. He'd done it two years ago. Brent had gotten a call from his aunt on his mother's side. Albert Clarkson had left this world by way of a self-inflicted gunshot wound to the head. He'd done it while drunk off his ass, sitting in a recliner in his then-girlfriend's trailer.

Brent had not gone to the funeral. He'd essentially hung up on any family member that had called to check up on him. He wasn't blind to the fact that his desire to kill these women had not come until after his father's suicide. The asshole killing himself had brought all of those old memories back. Memories of walking or even riding his bike down to the old country store to steal booze for his dad. Getting beaten like a dog if he failed to bring something back. And even when his father *did* get his drink, he'd get angry after too much of it and still beat the hell out of him.

Oddly enough, though, Brent found himself thinking of the trips back to the house when he'd managed to steal the cheap liquor for his dad. He'd felt like he had accomplished something and that his father might finally be proud of him. Maybe he had done something that would finally make his father happy.

Even stranger was that he felt that same hopeful feeling as he watched the older FBI agent walking to the front door and back into the house. She knocked and the door was answered by Darla a few seconds later.

Brent held his breath when she disappeared into the house. The night was so quiet he could hear the latch clicking into place within the frame.

The anticipation came on fast and hard. Usually, it gathered slightly until it was overwhelming, something he compared to the world's longest build-up to orgasm. But this was better, this was longer lasting. He'd felt variations of it ever since he'd decided to start killing them. The first time, he'd almost felt as if he had gone too far. He knew that killing these girls for trying to drink underage—and, as such, trying to pull a fast one on him and get him into trouble—was a bit much, but they deserved it. And with each one he took down, he became more and more convinced that he was doing the world a favor. Hell, he was doing the girls a favor. He was sparing them a life that was headed in the direction of the life his miserable father had led.

He felt it as he stepped out of the trees and cut off at an angle to go into the back yard. He thought of taking her license earlier in the night, knowing damn well there was no way she was twenty-one.

He saw that picture of her in his mind's eye and focused on it.

When he reached under his windbreaker for the graduation cap, he lost himself for a moment. The night—and maybe even time itself—became fluid. For a moment, he was not reaching for a graduation cap but a bottle of Night Train that he had stolen for his father.

Weapon or liquor, he supposed it didn't matter.

In the end, they both meant death.

Chapter Twenty Nine

Kate was beginning to feel very had for Darla Dowdy. The poor girl was still a mess. She was worried about her parents finding out about her careless mistakes which, Kate thought, would eventually happen. There would be reports filed and named taken down. She didn't see any way this would all get wrapped up without the Dowdys finding out about it. Of course, Darla's main concern was her parents finding out that she had invited a complete stranger to deliver alcohol to their home. It was a valid concern; Kate still couldn't believe the girl had done such a thing.

"You okay?" Kate asked.

"Yeah. This is all... just a bit much. And I'm tired. But there's no way in hell I'm going to sleep."

Kate figured casual conversation might help to ease the girl's mind. Kate fished for something as she looked out the living room window. They had left the porch light on to deter anyone from possibly stalking across the front yard.

"I take it you were home from college for Thanksgiving break?" Kate asked.

"Yeah."

"Where do you go to school?"

"Virginia Tech."

"And given that you were having someone buy and deliver alcohol, I assume you're not yet twenty-one?"

"Nope. Six whole months short."

"Do the college bars tend to let you get away with it?"

"Sometimes. I've tried it three times and it worked twice. I guess I got cocky tonight. Cocky and pissed off at my friends."

Kate found herself wanting to ask what in the hell she'd been thinking, inviting a man she did not know to her house at such an hour. But she wasn't about to lecture a kid that was not her own. And honestly, if she wanted Darla calm, that was absolutely not going to be the best way to play it. She could remember that age, being on the precipice of becoming an adult and assuming you were close enough to get away with quite a bit. For some, it was just a number. To others, it was a sense of identity, she supposed.

Still, that instinct to nurture was strong. She couldn't remember the last time she'd felt it so strongly. She wondered if it had something to do with being a new mother, her body going through the change a mother went through in those first several months. Apparently, some things simply did not change with age.

"You want a drink or something?" Darla asked. She then grinned at herself and shook the comment away. "I meant like water or soda."

"Water would be great, actually."

Darla headed into the kitchen, leaving Kate alone in the living room. She looked through the window, into the night, and found herself aching for her own family.

⚜ ⚜ ⚜

Brent approached the back porch and looked through the window. The living room light was on and he could catch little glimpses of movement here and there. He figured the back door along the porch was locked, so that was going to be a useless way in. He hugged tightly to the side of the house, holding the graduation cap in his hands.

The last two girls he had killed, he'd managed to do it right at their front door. With Kayla, it had been accidental. It had just been a matter of good timing. But there had been something poetic about it—about this drunken harlot, coming back home after leaving, going to college and coming back. Thinking she was better than this town, better than him. Thinking she could flash her ID and because she'd set out to make something of herself that he'd just do whatever she wanted.

He'd loved the idea of killing them at their front door so much that he'd made sure to do it that way with Vanessa Fenton. He'd planned on doing the very same thing with Darla Dowdy, too, but she had come home early. When he arrived too late and saw that her parents weren't home, he planned on simply knocking on her door. But then the guy with the beer had showed up and ruined that as well.

So he was just going to have to get it done any way he could. He'd broken into homes before. The first time, he'd been fourteen years old and had stolen his friend's Barry Sanders rookie card. Then, at sixteen, he'd broken into an ex-girlfriend's house and stolen some bras and panties. He loved the voyeurism of it but had never had the guile and stealth to get very involved with it.

Knowing that Darla's parents weren't home was a huge help. All he had to do was find a window somewhere on the backside of the house, as far away from the living room as he could. And, to his delight, he came across such a window mere seconds after passing by the back porch. The window sat about four feet off the ground. There were blinds on the inside, partially cracked open.

He placed his fist inside of the graduation cap and felt his heart racing. He had to hit the glass hard enough to break it, but gently enough so that when he did break it, he did not rattle the blinds on the other side. He drew his arm back and punched forward quickly. All he got was a small sliver of a crack for his efforts.

He grimaced and punched again. This time the glass fractured and broke, splintering inward. He pushed against it and most of it fell inward. It wasn't a very big section, but large enough to put his arm into. His only problem would be the stupid blinds.

Carefully, he reached in through the broken glass. Little shards of glass pricked and scraped him as he reached up, looking for the lock latch. His fingers slid across it, then grasped it, then turned.

Glass dug into his arm. It brought a memory of his father to mind like a bolt of lightning. His father, screaming. Drunk, wobbling, throwing punches. Mad because Brent had gotten caught trying to steal a bottle of Night Train from the store down the road. Calling him useless, slapping him and punching him.

Brent had felt useless most of his life. If he ever sat down on a couch with a shrink, he supposed they'd easily figure out his feelings of uselessness had stemmed from the way his father had treated him. But those were simply the cards he had been dealt and he had played them as well he could.

Brent snapped out of that memory, wincing at the pain of the glass digging into his skin. He drew his arm back out, paying no attention to the little pin pricks of blood on his forearm. He pressed against the edges of the window and pushed up. The window slid in its frame easily, almost as if it wanted him to get inside.

⚜ ⚜ ⚜

It had been eleven minutes since DeMarco had left. Kate had no idea how long it might take for DeMarco, Gates, and his officers to find Brent Clarkson. She could be out of here within the next few minutes, or she could very well be here when the sun came up. It made the situation between her and Darla rather awkward, but necessary.

Darla kept looking at her phone, scrolling through Facebook. The girl now looked almost heartbroken. Given everything the night had dumped on her, Kate wondered if Darla was missing her parents.

"Do you need to call your folks?" Kate asked.

"No. They'd freak out. Especially my mom."

Understandably so, she thought, but did not say out loud.

She checked her watch, somehow shocked to find that it was just a little after one o'clock in the morning. She was getting tired, her leg was aching like crazy, and truth be told, she just wanted this to all be over. She wanted to wrap this case, get back home, and have a long conversation with Allen about what their futures were going to look like.

"I'm curious," Kate said. "Tonight when you had tried getting drinks at Pauly's had you ever attempted to get drinks there before?"

"No. I got desperate. All of my friends went out drinking in Charlotte and I was depressed."

"They're of age, I take it."

"Yes. And like I said, tonight was the first time I ever tried it."

"Had you seen the bartender before?"

"Yeah, he's all over the place. Brent something, I think. Some of the girls make a pretty big fuss over him."

Kate nodded, having already heard this. It did make her sad to think some girls believed they could get away with anything when they were pretty enough and if there was a handsome man involved.

"Can you excuse me just a second?" Darla said. "I need to go to the bathroom."

Kate nodded. There was a waver in the girl's voice, a slight break that made Kate fairly certain she was only escaping to the bathroom to have some private time to cry. Kate could remember being twenty, somewhat removed from her family and still not quite sure who her friends were. Of course, she'd also had her mind and heart firmly set on a career within the FBI and she had placed all of her uncertainty and anxiety on that. Maybe Darla didn't have anything like that.

Kate drank the last of the water Darla had given her and headed into the adjoining kitchen. She placed the glass in the sink and looked through the kitchen window. The night seemed even darker in the back yard, a perfect square of darkness. It made Kate feel uneasy, so she reached out and flipped on the light switch she assumed was for the back porch.

It came on, illuminating a modest little porch. For a silly moment, she almost expected the killer to be out there, peering through the glass at her. Her heart actually sprinted in her chest a bit at this thought.

Just as she got control of her overactive nerves, she realized that she *could* see something in the glass, though. It was murky and made no sense at first. She glared into the glass and then, a split moment too late, she realized what she was seeing.

She *was* seeing the killer. Only he wasn't outside lurking on the porch.

He was behind her.

Chapter Thirty

Kate reached for her Glock and wheeled around as quickly as she could. She caught a hard right-handed jab to the cheek for her efforts. She stutter-stepped backward, her hand still going for her gun. As her hand fell on the butt of it, though, the killer was on her. He slammed hard against her, catching her between his body and the kitchen counter. He pressed against her back, pushing her hard into the granite countertop.

And then she felt the soft graze of something around her neck. Because she knew what it was, it may as well have been razor wire, cutting through her neck. Just as she realized what was happening, she felt herself being pulled backward by the neck. He pulled hard, causing her to gag right away. He gave such a brutal tug on the cord that held the tassels in place that her feet left the ground for a moment.

She knew not to panic. It would only make her run out of breath sooner. But the strength with which he was tugging back made her fear that he may actually be able to snap her neck—probably not with the tassels and cord, but perhaps with just his strength alone.

With the cord digging into her neck and his weight behind her, Kate did her best to relax. Her toes finally settled back down and touched the floor. She sagged, making it harder for him to support her weight. When he repositioned himself and adjusted, Kate acted as quickly as she could. She felt like she was moving in slow motion as she rocketed her legs up, placing them against the cabinets under the kitchen sink.

For a moment, the cord and tassels were unbearably right around her neck. But in that same moment, Kate pushed herself off of the cabinets as hard as she could. The killer was expecting it but had not been able to brace himself fast enough.

They both went falling backward. There was an enormous clatter of noise as Brent Clarkson collided with one of the chairs by the kitchen table. Kate felt the wind go out of him and heard him grunt as he rebounded from the chair, knocking it over and slamming onto the floor.

The grip around her neck loosened considerably and she was able to pull away from him. As she did, though, he reached out and grabbed her hair, pulling her back down.

While all of this happened, Kate heard Darla's voice. "Agent Wise?"

The girl was rushing out of the bathroom, apparently drawn out by all of the commotion. Her voice alerted both Kate and Brent; they both looked at her at the same time. The only difference was that Kate had been trained to shut out such distractions. With her hair still wrapped in Brent's grip, she attacked the only way she could in that moment.

She threw her head back so hard she felt the strain of muscles in her neck. The back of her head collided with his face, smashing into his mouth and nose. She then wheeled around, still partially on top of him, and delivered a punch to his throat. He looked surprised as he coughed and gagged. But he was not fazed enough to simply lie there while she went for her gun, When she went to remove it, he brought a hard left hand toward her face. It was slow and lumbering, allowing her to block it easily. But it also gave him the chance to push her off of him.

She went skidding into the kitchen table, nearly knocking it over. It rattled and shook, the salt and pepper shakers coming down to thump on the floor beside her. Something else fell as well, some decorative vase with little glass pearls and beads inside of it. It nearly clocked her in the head when it fell, but instead struck the linoleum floor with a solid *thunk*.

As Kate tried to pick herself up, she saw that Darla was charging at Brent. She was coming up behind him and he had no idea she was advancing. The girl couldn't weigh any more than one hundred pounds, but when she threw herself hard at the back of his knees, she did so with tremendous force. Brent stumbled forward but caught himself mid-fall on the edge of the table. He turned to face Darla, sneering at her through a small stream of blood caused by Kate's backwards headbutt. Brent struck her hard with an open-handed slap that sent the girl to the floor.

Kate went for her gun again. She pulled it and was in the process of bringing it up when Brent kicked at her arms. Kate, in a kneeling position, was knocked over by the force of the kick. Worse than that, her gun went clattering to the floor, sliding further out into the kitchen.

Brent was apparently done trying to take his time and stick to his usual means of murder via the graduation cap. He leaped for the gun in an impressively athletic move. He moved fast—so fast that Kate was not able to respond until his hand was on the gun and he was pulling it to himself.

"Darla, run," Kate said.

Kate then did the only thing she could think to do. It felt stupid, given her age and the physical specimen she was fighting against. From her kneeling position, she half-jumped onto Brent's back, planting a knee as hard as she could into his lower back. He howled in pain but his grip never left the gun. In fact, his finger inched closer to the trigger as he bucked her off of him.

She stumbled back, desperate and starting to feel terror sink into her nerves. Brent was rolling over onto his back, bringing the gun with him. Kate knew she was going to have to act in any way she could, even if it was by ridiculous measures. She reached for the overturned chair beside her, intending to use it as a shield. When she did, she saw the vase of glass pebbles and beads. She recalled the heavy sound it had made when it had struck the floor and did not break.

She grabbed the leg of the chair with her left hand and then took the vase with the right. In front of her, Brent was on his back, leveling the gun at her. She whipped the chair as hard as she could at him, but it really only slid against his leg. Still, it was enough to cause him to have to readjust the gun.

Kate took her moment, knowing that if she didn't succeed, she and Darla Dowdy would both be dead within seconds.

She hefted the vase in her hand and chucked it like a throwing knife. It glittered, end over end, spilling its decorative contents along the way. The beads and pebbles striking the floor sounded almost musical. The sound of the vase slamming into Brent Clarkson's head was not. If her headbutt had not broken his nose, the vase did.

He reacted out of instinct, his hands going to his face, the right one still holding the gun. Kate knew her risks were far from over, but she had to act. She sprang forward, partially slipping on some of the glass pebbles, and grabbed his right hand with both of hers. She then trapped it between her breast and her clutched hands, giving it a hard twist.

It was harder than she expected. She felt something in Brent's wrist move far more than it should have. She had not meant to use that much force, but the adrenaline coursing through her veins was like gasoline.

Brent screamed and dropped the gun. She could see his eyes growing hazy and she wondered if the vase had maybe struck him hard enough to cause a concussion. Blood coursed down his cheek as he struck out with his left hand. He was so enraged and in pain that he had forgotten he no longer had the gun and only one hand to fight with.

Kate could have somehow cuffed him. It would have hurt him terribly, but she could have done it.

But something in her was twisting and darkening, like a storm cloud rolling up on a rural field. She reached down and grabbed the vase again. It was smeared with his blood and there was a crack doing down the top of it.

"What do you…" Brent said, but that was all he got out.

Kate brought the vase around one more time, swinging it hard with her right hand. It struck him along the brow, the back side of it shattering and spilling the rest of the pebbles and beads onto the floor.

Brent Clarkson fell back to the floor as if he had fallen asleep. There was a sickening moment where Kate feared she had killed him, but she could see the labored rise and fall of his chest within seconds.

Kate got to her feet and nearly fell over. She had managed to aggravate whatever she had pulled in her right leg. It flared up in pain whenever she tried to use that leg. Seeing Kate's difficulty, Darla pulled over one of the other chairs from the other side of the table.

"Are you okay?" Darla asked. Her voice was thin and tired. The girl seemed to be on the verge of a breakdown.

"Yes," Kate said, taking out her phone. "Could you please very carefully bring me the gun?"

Darla nodded. She took two huge steps to the gun, keeping her eyes on the unconscious Brent Clarkson the entire time. She carried the gun with two hands as she brought it over to Kate. Kate took it and held it in her right hand. With her left, she pulled up DeMarco's number and placed the call.

She answered right away, sounding out of breath. "Yeah?" she asked. "What's up, Kate?"

"I sort of have Brent Clarkson."

"What?"

"Yeah. He broke into the house and tried to strangle me."

"Oh my God, Kate, are you okay?"

"Yeah. A little shook up."

"And Darla?"

"The same. Clarkson is knocked out. I don't know for how long. You might want to get here as soon as you can."

She could hear movement, as well as murmured voices, in the background. "I'm already on the way," DeMarco said.

Chapter Thirty One

It was 4:15, and Kate was chugging down a cup of bitter coffee with far too much sugar. She had the jitters and her stomach felt like a boiling pool of lava. But she was doing her best to keep all of that hidden. She was, after all, sitting across from Brent Clarkson. He'd been looked over by a medic and would soon be on his way to the hospital. He had a fractured nose, a dislocated wrist, and a concussion to go along with the goose egg Kate had placed on his forehead with the aid of the Dowdys' decorative vase.

The strange thing was that neither Kate nor DeMarco had requested this meeting. As far as they were concerned, the case was closed and Clarkson could heal up in the hospital before gearing up for what would be a very short trial. No, it was Clarkson who had asked to speak with them.

They'd been sitting like this, DeMarco and Kate on one side of the interrogation table and Clarkson on the other, for about a minute. So far, Clarkson had said nothing. He was taking breaths through his mouth, as taking them through his cracked nose seemed to cause him discomfort. Kate was aware of DeMarco's gaze on her, making sure she was okay. Kate honestly had no problem with the way she had handled Clarkson even though that last blast to the head with the vase might be seen by some as unnecessary. But she *was* feeling out of sorts. It wasn't just her stomach or the fact that she was tired. It was her nerves. She was anxious and sad and, if she boiled it all down to the root of the matter, she wanted to be home with Michael and Allen.

"I'm not crazy," Brent said finally. "I'm not some psychotic or maniac."

"I can think of several psychologists who might disagree," DeMarco said.

"I'm sure both of you think it was out of jealousy, right? The washed up bartender, coming up on the exit of his prime, acting out on prissy, snobby girls that went off to college and came back home, thinking they were so much better than everyone."

"Yes, it had crossed our minds," DeMarco said. Kate was glad DeMarco was being so vocal. She wasn't sure she had it in her to speak. Hell, she found it hard to look at Brent Clarkson. She could still feel his wrist dislocating beneath her hands and it made the stress within her stomach that much worse.

"It was my father," he said. "I think I realized it while I was walking across the back yard to break into the Dowdy house. I was killing these girls because I wasn't able to kill my father. I saw in them what destroyed the man who raised me and I wanted it dead. I wanted to kill it. And these young girls were already so desperate for attention and seeking something to numb themselves that—"

"Stop," DeMarco said. "You killed three young women and were going for a fourth. I don't care what your father did, I don't care if your father was Hitler. I'm not going to listen to your excuses. So unless you have some better reason for wanting to speak with us, Agent Wise and I would like to get home."

Kate finished the rest of her coffee in response to this. She then looked to Clarkson and started speaking before she was aware there were any words on her tongue.

"I've been doing this for over thirty years," she said. "I've heard every excuse in the book, from the mouths of killers and their therapists. Daddy was never there. Mommy never loved me. Daddy hit mommy. Kids teased me. I was abused. I've heard it all, Mr. Clarkson. And you know what? Sometimes those traumas do terribly demented things to a person's mind. I recognize that and, as hard as it is to accept sometimes, I concede that. But what you've done in this town—you've taken daughters from their parents. You've taken a small community's sense of safety. And you did it with a graduation cap from the high school you graduated from. That speaks of forethought and intent. It speaks of a man that kills because he likes it. I don't give a damn if your father drank himself into a coma on a nightly basis. It's an excuse. And I'm just sad that I won't be around to see a judge tell you the same thing."

That said, she glared at him a moment longer. She took in the lump on his head, the misshapen state of his nose and the dried blood that had been poorly wiped off. She'd done that, and now that it was all over, she wished she could have done more. She felt tears coming on for reasons she could not grasp in that moment. She turned quickly and exited the room.

She instantly rushed to the back of the building, toward the break room. She got a bottle of water out of the staff fridge and sipped from it slowly. She pressed her head against the wall, tilting slightly to keep the weight off of her aching right leg, and took a series of deep breaths.

"Kate?"

She turned her head to the right and saw DeMarco standing there. "I'm okay. Sorry about that outburst."

"No need to apologize. But are you sure you're okay?"

"Yeah. I just..."

She knew what she wanted to say, but saying it was going to break her heart. Instead, she asked: "Should we check in with Gates?"

"No need. He just now texted me. He's still with Darla Dowdy and has spoken with her parents. They'll be home at ten tomorrow morning. Gates has said that between himself and Smith, they can make sure someone is there with Darla until they get home." She hesitated here and then took a few steps closer. "What were you going to say, Kate? You just what?"

Kate looked at DeMarco, a woman who had somehow become her friend aside from her partner over the past two years.

"I just want to go home."

It was a heavy comment and when she voiced it, Kate Wise felt as if an immense weight had been unfastened from her heart. And when she finally allowed herself a few tears in front of DeMarco, it was like drawing open a shade that had been closed for years to let the sun shine through.

⚜ ⚜ ⚜

"Forgive me, but I have to ask."

DeMarco was sitting behind the wheel, closing in on DC. It was a little after noon; Kate figured that after a debrief with Duran, she would be stepping foot into her home in Richmond sometime after three. She'd FaceTimed with Allen and Michael—needing to see her little baby's sweet face—before they'd left Harper Hills, and the level of excitement in her heart was akin to that of a teenager going to visit her crush for the first time in forever.

Kate considered DeMarco's question. She knew what her partner was about to ask and though she did not want to talk about it, she figured she owed DeMarco that much, at least.

"Of course you can," she finally answered.

"After all of this—after our moment back there in the break room in Harper Hills PD—do you really think that's it?"

She nearly said yes, but if her career had taught her anything, it was to never be so sure. Yet when she thought of the coming years with Allen and her new son, that yes seemed to glow in neon. But rather than give such a direct answer, she instead said: "It feels like it."

"If it is, I'd say you went out on a high note. Brent Clarkson was a beefy hunk of a man and you handed him his ass. I'd add in your age to the end of that, but I think you've had enough of that in the past few months, right?"

"That's correct." She snickered here and then added, "Though if I'm being totally honest with you, I never really minded being the Miracle Mom."

"Being? You still are. Milk that cow for all it's worth!"

They had a laugh over this, and Kate silently thanked DeMarco for letting the question go so easily. She looked out the window, the afternoon bright and warm. Thanksgiving was two days away and she knew that for a few families back in Harper Hills, it would be a painful and heartbreaking holiday.

It made her feel more thankful for what she had waiting for her at home and, perhaps more importantly, all the many twists and turns along the path that had led her there.

Chapter Thirty Two

Kate learned another thing about Allen two days later, during Thanksgiving: the man cooked the juiciest turkey she'd ever tasted. And that was a good thing because his mashed potatoes were lumpy and he burned two of the four pies they had made together. The turkey was the centerpiece of the Thanksgiving dinner that filled her kitchen counters. While the counters were filled with food, her kitchen table was filled with people. And as she stood up to say grace, she took in the sight of all of those people and her heart felt so full it could burst.

Michael was sitting in his highchair, situated between her chair and Allen. Melissa sat on the other side of the table with her husband, Terry, and Michelle following suit. Sitting at the far end of the table, DeMarco looked a little uncomfortable. She'd griped about being the only single one at the dinner but had appreciated the invitation far too much to decline.

Kate said grace, doing her best to actually make it a memorable one. While her own thoughts on God were murky, she did not see the sense in that cheapening her thankfulness. She spoke earnestly for about two minutes, head bowed and eyes closed, and nearly caught herself crying on two different occasions.

The feast that followed was extraordinary. It wasn't just the food (though that played a big part), but the company. Everyone gelled well, even Terry, who had always tended to be a little too introverted for Kate's tastes. But as Michelle had gotten older, Terry had started to come out of his shell. He was a good father and Kate was finally convinced that he was an amazing husband to Melissa.

Conversation floated from work, to movies, to politics. Two bottles of wine were drained as a third was popped open. With dinner done, DeMarco brought out her contribution to the dinner, a pineapple upside down cake. "I know it's not a Thanksgiving staple," she quipped. "But screw you guys; it's the only dessert I know how to make and it's delicious."

When the meal was over, the men ordered the women to sit in the living room while they did the dishes. DeMarco smirked at this as she, Kate, and Melissa walked into the living room. She was holding Michael, while Kate held Melissa. "Those are some good men," DeMarco said with a laugh.

"Yeah, I guess we'll keep them," Melissa said.

When they settled down in the living room, Kate was amazed at how normal it felt. She'd spent so long wrestling to keep her professional and family life apart that she'd always expected it would be awkward to have DeMarco meet her family. While DeMarco had been to her house a few times in the past and had met Melissa, there was something different about it now. There was no tension or worry within her. Not even when DeMarco spoke up and essentially put her on blast—in a good-natured sort of way.

"So, Melissa, what's it going to take to keep your mother staying away from the FBI?"

Melissa laughed heartily at this but managed to get out an answer. "An act of God. Or maybe when she gets old enough where she has to wear adult diapers. I think she might call it quits by then."

"You wish," Kate said.

"How's the leg?" DeMarco asked.

"Stiff. So when I insert it into your backside, it won't bend going in."

Kate knew her partner was only ribbing her so she was able to take it on the chin in good fun. The three of them had a good laugh together as they cooed and spoke to the babies. But as she looked over to DeMarco, she saw something like worry buried in her partner's expression.

It wasn't until later, when Kate walked DeMarco out to her car, that she brought that look up. Night was falling and DeMarco looked rather anxious to get back to DC.

"Did you enjoy it?" Kate asked.

"Oh, Kate, this was beautiful. Much nicer than the awkward silences I would have endured at my parents' place. It's not just the sexuality part of it; they have no problems asking for elaborate details about recent cases. And given what we just went through, I couldn't have done that."

"Well, you're welcome any time. So long as you're always honest with me." She said this last part giving a playful little nudge.

"What's that supposed to mean?"

"It means I know something is bothering you."

When DeMarco looked back at her, she was in tears. "I'm torn," she said. "Kate, I don't know where I'd be in my career right now without you. You've been a great friend and mentor. And an amazing partner. But you were different this time, out in Harper Hills. I could tell you were distracted... that you were also torn. I would love nothing more than for you to be by my side until the day you die but... I also want you to enjoy the rest of your life. And I think... I think I know the decision you'll be making in the next few days."

Kate stepped forward and embraced her. "I do have a decision to make. And you just spent the afternoon with the group of people I will be thinking about when I make that decision. So you can see the weight of it, right?"

"Yeah, I can see it."

They broke the embrace and DeMarco slowly got into her car. "Whatever you decide, I'll support you."

"I know you will."

"Can I ask one favor, though?"

"Of course."

"If you decide that you're done and you won't be coming back to the bureau, will you make a point to always invite me to Thanksgiving?"

Kate smiled and bit back a little sob. "You can count on that."

⚜ ⚜ ⚜

Kate was staring at Darla Dowdy, the girl's face a mask of absolute horror. She was weeping and there were twin scratch marks on both sides of her face. "You have to stop," Darla said.

"I can't stop."

Kate's voice was distant and monotone, the voice of an expressionless drone. There was no emotion, no inflection. She was holding the glass vase that had fallen from the table. It was partially cracked, a small hole in the bottom allowing the contents to come spilling out. Only they weren't glass pebbles and beads now. Instead, they were rocks plucked from a river, stained with blood and flesh.

"Please..." Darla said. "It's over."

"Never over," Kate said.

"But you saved me," Darla said. "I'm safe now, so you can stop."

"But there are others," Kate said. "There will always be others."

"You're right," Darla said. "There will always be others that need saving. But there are others to do that now. Your time is over, Agent Wise."

Kate felt her muscles loosening, the vase growing heavy in her hands. She dropped it and when it crashed to the floor, it shattered into a million little crystals. The crystals covered the floor like little pebbles and in each one there was a face of someone she had saved over the course of her thirty-year career.

She saw the face of a six-year-old girl she had saved from a delusional stepfather in 1994. She saw the faces of three people who had been held hostage in a gym for three days, a case she had cracked in 2004. There were abused wives, innocent people that were thought to be guilty, people running from danger . . . too many faces to count. She had saved them all during her time with the bureau, and though many of the faces were murky, she held the shapes and details in her mind.

"You can let it go now," Darla said from behind her.

Kate jerked awake so fast she was dizzy for a moment as she sat up in bed. Her heart was pounding as the last remnants of the nightmare swept through her head.

"What is it?" Allen asked. "Bad dream?"

"I don't know," she said. A smile tickled the corners of her mouth as she lay back down. "Maybe, I think . . . maybe it was a good dream."

Allen sat up, rubbing at his eyes with one hand while placing his other arm around her. "You need to talk about it?"

"Eventually. But not right now."

She briefly thought of DeMarco, how she had called her out on needing to make a decision just before she'd left after Thanksgiving. That had been eight days ago and there was still no decision made. She and Allen had talked about it here and there, but there had been nothing solid.

"You sure?" Allen asked again.

"Yeah. Go back to sleep. I'm okay."

Allen kissed her on the shoulder and then lay back down. Slowly, Kate lay down next to him, spooning herself against him. She was tired, lingering in that zone of almost-asleep with Allen next to her. Her arm was around him, her hand planted on his chest. He nestled into her and turned slightly. When he did, she kissed him on the base of the neck. He turned even more and she allowed her hand to venture further down.

They were making love thirty seconds later. It was slow, it was sweet, and it was relatively quick. They lay together afterward and Kate allowed herself a moment to cry against his shoulder. He held her tight and once again, Kate felt her heart fill up.

It should be enough to make her upcoming decision easier.

But that turned out not to be the case.

⚜ ⚜ ⚜

It was one thing to push a stroller with her granddaughter in it, but quite another to push one with her son in it. Kate could not explain why, but it was an altogether different experience. She pushed it through the small Christmas tree lot in Carytown, filing down the aisles of trees and taking in the scent of pine and spruce.

Melissa was walking beside her, pushing Michelle. It was December fifth, and they were shopping for a tree for Melissa's house. Kate was perfectly happy with the fake one that had been in her attic for the past twenty years, but Melissa was insisting on a real one for her family this year. They would stop to look at one, study it, and then move on around the time Michelle would start to reach out and bat at the branches with her pudgy hand.

"I got a call from one of the local news stations today," Kate said. "And one from one of those nationwide pre-primetime news shows, two days ago."

"They still milking the Miracle Mom angle?"

"Very much. They were asking about a potential Miracle Mom Christmas. Wanting to know what Christmas would look like in Miracle Mom's house."

"And you turned them down, didn't you?"

"I turned down the nationwide one. But the local guys will be showing up on the twenty-third to do an interview."

"Good for you, Mom."

"There's something else I need to tell you, too." She said it with the sort of tone that usually came followed by a statement like *you might want to sit down.*

Melissa stopped pushing her stroller. Her face was mostly blank. Kate assumed it was because she wasn't sure where this was going. "Good or bad?"

"Depends," she said. "Director Duran called me last week."

"Mom . . . you don't have to check in with me."

"And I told him I'm done."

A smile lit up Melissa's face but she quickly tried to hide it. "And you're okay with that?"

"I think I am. I'm three years away from being sixty years old. I have a granddaughter and, somehow, a newborn son."

"How'd he take it?"

"Fine. I think he was expecting it. He did ask if I would consider staying on under a freelance basis to help with research and profiling assistance. I told him as long as it could all be done remotely, I'd consider it. So that's where I'm at now."

"So I bet Allen is happy with this news?" Melissa asked, starting to walk again.

"Yes. We've already started planning a week-long vacation sometime in the first part of next year to celebrate. Think you'd be up to babysitting for us?"

"I'd love to."

They continued on, walking by a trio of carolers that were situated among the trees. In the midst of their rendition of "Hark the Herald Angels" it was Melissa's turn to drop a bombshell.

"He's going to ask you to marry him. You know that, right?"

Kate smiled and nodded. "I hope so."

"I can tell it by the way he looks at you. At the risk of sounding like a know-it-all, I think he was just waiting to see how much longer you'd choose the job first."

It stung to hear it, but she knew it was true. "Melissa, I'm very sorry if I made you feel second. I know I did at many points during your life—especially after your father died. You deserved better."

Melissa shrugged. "Maybe I did. But the decisions you made turned you into who you are today. And I have to admit, you're pretty awesome the way you are."

"Yeah, I guess I sort of am," Kate said, playfully kicking at her daughter.

They continued on through the Christmas tree farm. Melissa finally decided on one fifteen minutes later. As the men at the farm bundled it up and placed it on the back of Allen's borrowed truck, Kate thought of her daughter decorating it, starting family traditions that Kate had fallen through on for so many years.

But all of that was over now. And though Kate was a realist and realized that she may only have about twenty-five years of life ahead of her—if she was lucky—it was a bright and promising future. It was a future she finally had full control over, no regrets and nothing to hold her back.

She was the Miracle Mom to some. She was a normal mother to Melissa. And someday soon, maybe she'd be a wife again.

She could be many things now, unburdened by a career that she had placed so high above everything else. She figured she could look into the rearview mirror of life to check on it every now and then, to remind her of where she had been—and perhaps more importantly, where she was headed.

A New Series!
Now Available for Pre-Order!

LEFT TO DIE
(An Adele Sharp Mystery–Book One)

"When you think that life cannot get better, Blake Pierce comes up with another masterpiece of thriller and mystery! This book is full of twists and the end brings a surprising revelation. I strongly recommend this book to the permanent library of any reader that enjoys a very well written thriller."

—Books and Movie Reviews, Roberto Mattos (re Almost Gone)

LEFT TO DIE is book #1 in a new FBI thriller series by USA Today bestselling author Blake Pierce, whose #1 bestseller Once Gone (Book #1) (a free download) has received over 1,000 five star reviews.

FBI special agent Adele Sharp is a German-and-French raised American with triple citizenship—and an invaluable asset in bringing criminals to justice as they cross American and European borders.

When a serial killer case spanning three U.S. states goes cold, Adele returns to San Francisco and to the man she hopes to marry. But after a shocking twist, a new lead surfaces and Adele is dispatched to Paris, to lead an international manhunt.

Adele returns to the Europe of her childhood, where familiar Parisian streets, old friends from the DGSI and her estranged father reignite her dormant obsession with solving her own mother's murder. All the while she must hunt down the diabolical killer, must enter the dark canals of his psychotic mind to know where he will strike next—and save the next victim before it's too late.

An action-packed mystery series of international intrigue and riveting suspense, LEFT TO DIE will have you turning pages late into the night.

Books #2 and #3 in the series – LEFT TO RUN and LEFT TO HIDE – are also available for preorder!

LEFT TO DIE
(An Adele Sharp Mystery–Book One)

Did you know that I've written multiple novels in the mystery genre? If you haven't read all my series, click the image below to download a series starter!

Made in the USA
Las Vegas, NV
06 April 2021

20892923R00111